A
GHOSTLY
GRAVE

The Man in the Mirror

Once the chains were unhooked from the coffin and the excavator was out of the way, Jack Henry and I guided the coffin on the church truck into the back of my hearse. Before I shut the door, I had a sick feeling that someone was watching me. Of course the crowd was still there, but I mean someone was watching *my* every move.

I looked back over my shoulder toward the trailer park. The man in the John Deere hat popped out of sight behind the tree when he saw me look at him.

I shut the hearse door and got into the driver's side. Before I left the cemetery, I looked in my rearview mirror at the tree. The man was standing there. This time the shadow of the hat didn't hide his eyes.

We locked eyes.

"Look away," Chicken Teater warned me when he appeared in the passenger seat.

By Tonya Kappes

TONYA KAPPES

A GHOSTLY GRAVE

A GHOSTLY SOUTHERN MYSTERY

WITNESS

An Imprint of HarperCollinsPublishers

This book was originally published in 2013 in slightly different form and in e-book format.

WITNESS

An Imprint of HarperCollins*Publishers*
195 Broadway
New York, New York 10007

Copyright © 2013, 2015 by Tonya Kappes
Excerpt from *A Ghostly Demise* copyright © 2015 by Tonya Kappes
ISBN 978-0-06-237481-3
www.witnessimpulse.com

First Witness mass market printing: April 2015

HarperCollins ® is a registered trademark of HarperCollins Publishers.

Printed in the United States of America

10 9 8 7 6 5 4 3 2 1

Chapter 1

Just think, this all started because of Santa Claus. I took a drink of my large Diet Coke Big Gulp that I had picked up from the Buy and Fly gas station on the way over to Sleepy Hollow Cemetery to watch Chicken Teater's body being exhumed from his eternal resting place—only he was far from restful.

Damn Santa. I sucked up a mouthful of Diet Coke and swallowed. *Damn Santa.*

No, I didn't mean the real jolly guy with the belly shaking like a bowlful of jelly who leaves baby dolls and toy trucks; I meant the plastic light-up ornamental kind that people stick in their front yards during Christmas. The particular plastic Santa I was talking about was the one that had fallen off the roof of Artie's Deli and Meat just as I happened to walk under it, knocking me flat out cold.

Santa didn't give me anything but a bump on the head and the gift of seeing ghosts—let me be more specific—ghosts of people who have been murdered. They called me the Betweener medium, at least that was what the psychic from Lexington told us . . . *us* . . . *sigh* . . . I looked over at Jack Henry.

The Ray Ban sunglasses covered up his big brown eyes, which were the exact same color as a Hershey's chocolate bar. I looked into his eyes. And as with a chocolate bar, once I stared at them, I was a goner. Lost, in fact.

Today I was positive his eyes would be watering from the stench of a casket that had been buried for four years—almost four years to the day, now that I thought about it.

Jack Henry, my boyfriend and Sleepy Hollow sheriff, motioned for John Howard Lloyd to drop the claw that was attached to the tractor and begin digging. John Howard, my employee at Eternal Slumber Funeral Home, didn't mind digging up the grave. He dug it four years ago, so why not? He hummed a tune, happily chewing—gumming, since he had no teeth—a piece of straw he had grabbed up off the ground before he took his post behind the tractor controls. If someone who didn't know him came upon John Howard, they'd think he was a serial killer, with his dirty overalls, wiry hair and gummy smile.

The buzz of a moped scooter caused me to look back at the street. There was a crowd that had gathered behind the yellow police line to see what was happening because it wasn't every day someone's body was plucked from its resting place.

"Zula Fae Raines Payne, get back here!" an officer scolded my granny, who didn't pay him any attention. She waved her handkerchief in the air with one hand while she steered her moped right on through the police tape. "This is a crime scene and you aren't allowed over there."

Granny didn't even wobble but held the moped steady when she snapped right through the yellow tape.

"Woo hoooo, Emma!" Granny hollered, ignoring the officer, who was getting a little too close to her. A black helmet snapped on the side covered the top of her head, giving her plenty of room to sport her large black-rimmed sunglasses. She twisted the handle to full throttle. The officer took off at a full sprint to catch up to her. He put his arm out to grab her. "I declare!" Granny jerked her head back. "I'm Zula Raines Payne, the owner of Eternal Slumber, and this is one of my clients!"

"Ma'am, I know who you are. With all due respect, because my momma and pa taught me to respect my elders—and I do respect you, Ms. Payne—I can't let you cross that tape. You are going to have to go back behind the line!" He ran behind her and pointed to the yellow tape that she had already zipped through. "This is a crime scene. Need I remind you that you turned over operations of your business to your granddaughter? And only *she* has the right to be on the other side of the line."

I curled my head back around to see what Jack Henry and John were doing and pretended the roar of the excavator was drowning out the sounds around me, including those of Granny screaming my name. Plus, I didn't want to get into any sort of argument with Granny, since half the town came out to watch the 7-A.M. exhumation, and the Auxiliary women were the first in line—and would be the first to be at the Higher Grounds Café, eating their scones, drinking their coffee and coming up with all sorts of reasons why we had exhumed the body.

I could hear them now. *Ever since Zula Fae left*

Emma Lee and Charlotte Rae in charge of Eternal Slumber, it's gone downhill, or my personal favorite, *I'm not going to lay my corpse at Eternal Slumber just to have that crazy Emma Lee dig me back up. Especially since she's got a case of the Funeral Trauma.*

The "Funeral Trauma." After the whole Santa incident, I told Doc Clyde I was having some sort of hallucinations and seeing dead people. He said I had been in the funeral business a little too long and seeing corpses all of my life had been traumatic.

Regardless, the officer was half right—me and my sister were in charge of Eternal Slumber. At twenty-eight, I had been an undertaker for only three years. But, I had been around the funeral home my whole life. It is the family business, one I didn't want to do until I turned twenty-five years old and decided I better keep the business going. *Some business.* Currently, Granny still owned Eternal Slumber, but my sister, Charlotte Rae, and I ran the joint.

My parents completely retired and moved to Florida. Thank God for Skype or I'd never see them. I guess Granny was semi-retired. I say semi-retired because she put her two cents in when she wanted to. Today she wanted to.

Some family business.

Granny brought the moped to an abrupt stop. She hopped right off and flicked the snap of the strap and pulled the helmet off along with her sunglasses. She hung the helmet on the handle-bars and the glasses dangled from the *V* in her sweater exactly where she wanted it to hang—between her boobs. Doc Clyde was there and Granny had him on the hook exactly where she wanted to keep him.

Her short flaming-red hair looked like it was on fire, with the morning sun beaming down as she used her fingers to spike it up a little more than usual. After all, she knew she had to look good because she was the center of attention—next to Chicken Teater's exhumed body.

The officer ran up and grabbed the scooter's handle. He knew better than to touch Granny.

"I am sure your momma and pa did bring you up right, but if you don't let me go . . ." Granny jerked the scooter toward her. She was a true Southern belle and put things in a way that no other woman could. I looked back at them and waved her over. The police officer stepped aside. Granny took her hanky out of her bra and wiped off the officer's shoulder like she was cleaning lint or something. "It was *lovely* to meet you." Granny's voice dripped like sweet honey. She put the hanky back where she had gotten it.

I snickered. *Lovely* wasn't always a compliment from a Southern gal. Like the gentleman he claimed to be, he took his hat off to Granny and smiled.

She didn't pay him any attention as she bee-lined it toward me.

"Hi," she said in her sweet Southern drawl, waving at everyone around us. She gave a little extra wink toward Doc Clyde. His cheeks rose to a scarlet red. Nervously, he ran his fingers through his thinning hair and pushed it to the side, defining the side part.

Everyone in town knew he had been keeping late hours just for Granny, even though she wasn't a bit sick. God knew what they were doing and I didn't want to know.

Granny pointed her hanky toward Pastor Brown who was there to say a little prayer when the casket was exhumed. Waking the dead wasn't high on anyone's priority list. Granny put the cloth over her mouth and leaning in, she whispered, "Emma Lee, you better have a good reason to be digging up Chicken Teater."

We both looked at the large concrete chicken gravestone. The small gold plate at the base of the stone statue displayed all of Colonel Chicken Teater's stats with his parting words: *Chicken has left the coop.*

"Why don't you go worry about the Inn." I suggested for her to leave and glanced over at John Howard. He had to be getting close to reaching the casket vault.

Granny gave me the stink eye.

"It was only a suggestion." I put my hands up in the air as a truce sign.

Granny owned, operated and lived at the only bed-and-breakfast in town, the Sleepy Hollow Inn, known as "the Inn" around here. Everyone loved staying at the large mansion, which sat at the foothills of the caverns and caves that made Sleepy Hollow a main attraction in Kentucky . . . besides horses and University of Kentucky basketball.

Sleepy Hollow was a small tourist town that was low on crime, and that was the way we liked it.

Sniff, sniff. Whimpers were coming from underneath the large black floppy hat.

Granny and I looked over at Marla Maria Teater, Chicken's wife. She had come dressed to the nines with her black V-neck dress hitting her curves in all the right places. The hat covered up the eyes she was dabbing.

Of course, when the police notified her that they had good reason to believe that Chicken didn't die of a serious bout of pneumonia but was murdered, Marla took to her bed as any mourning widower would. She insisted on being here for the exhumation. Jack Henry had warned Marla Maria to keep quiet about why the police were opening up the files on Chicken's death. If there was a murderer on the loose and it got around, it could possibly hurt the economy, and this was Sleepy Hollow's busiest time of the year.

Granny put her arm around Marla and winked at me over Marla's shoulder.

"Now, now. I know it's hard, honey, I've buried a few myself. Granted, I've never had any dug up though." Granny wasn't lying. She has been twice widowed and I was hoping she'd stay away from marriage a third time. Poor Doc Clyde, you'd have thought he would stay away from her since her track record was . . . well . . . deadly. "That's a first in this town." Granny gave Marla Maria the elbow along with a wink and a click of her tongue.

Maybe the third time was the charm.

"Who is buried here?" Granny let go of Marla

and stepped over to the smaller tombstone next to Chicken's.

"Stop!" Jack Henry screamed, waving his hands in the air. "Zula, move!"

Granny looked up and ducked just as John Howard came back for another bite of ground with the claw.

I would hate to have to bury Granny anytime soon.

"Lady Cluckington," Marla whispered, tilting her head to the side. Using her finger, she dabbed the driest eyes I had ever seen. "Our prize chicken. Well, she isn't dead *yet*."

I glanced over at her. Her tone caused a little suspicion to stir in my gut.

"She's not a chicken. She's a Spangled Russian Orloff Hen!" Chicken Teater appeared next to his grave. His stone looked small next to his six-foot-two frame. He ran his hand over the tombstone Granny had asked about. There was a date of birth, but no date of death. "You couldn't stand having another beauty queen in my life!"

"Oh no," I groaned and took another gulp of my Diet Coke. He—his ghost—was the last thing that I needed to see this morning.

"Is that sweet tea?" Chicken licked his lips. "I'd give anything to have a big ole sip of sweet tea."

He towered over me. His hair was neatly combed to the right; his red plaid shirt was tucked into his carpenter jeans.

This was the third time I had seen Chicken Teater since his death. It was a shock to the community to hear of a man passing from pneumonia in his early sixties. But that was what the doctors in Lexington said he died of, no questions asked, and his funeral was held at Eternal Slumber.

The first time I had seen Chicken Teater's ghost was after my perilous run-in with Santa. I too thought I was a goner, gone to the great beyond . . . but no . . . Chicken Teater and Ruthie Sue Payne— their ghosts anyway—stood right next to my hospital bed, eyeballing me. Giving me the onceover as if he was trying to figure out if I was dead or alive. Lucky for him I was alive and seeing him.

Ruthie Sue Payne was a client at Eternal Slumber who couldn't cross over until someone helped her solve her murder. That someone was me. The Betweener.

Since I could see her, talk to her, feel her and hear her, I was the one. Thanks to me, Ruthie's murder was solved and she was now resting peacefully on the other side. Chicken was a different story.

Apparently, Ruthie was as big of a gossip in the afterlife as she was in her earthly life. That was how Chicken Teater knew about me being a Betweener. Evidently, Ruthie was telling everyone about my special gift.

Chicken Teater wouldn't leave me alone until I agreed to investigate his death because he knew he didn't die from pneumonia. He claimed he was poisoned. But who would want to kill a chicken farmer?

Regardless, it took several months of me trying to convince Jack Henry there might be a possibility Chicken Teater was murdered. After some questionable evidence, provided by Chicken Teater, the case was reopened. I didn't understand all the red tape and legal yip-yap, but here we stood today.

Now it was time for me to get Chicken Teater to the other side.

"It's not dead yet?" Granny's eyebrows rose in amazement after Marla Maria confirmed there was an empty grave. Granny couldn't get past the fact there was a gravestone for something that wasn't dead.

I was still stuck on "prize chicken." What was a prize chicken?

A loud thud echoed when John Howard sent the claw down. There was an audible gasp from the crowd. The air was thick with anticipation. What did they think they were going to see?

Suddenly my nerves took a downward dive. What if the coffin opened? Coffin makers guaranteed they lock for eternity after they are sealed, but still, it wouldn't be a good thing for John Howard to pull the coffin up and have Chicken take a tumble next to Lady Cluckington's stone.

"I think we got 'er!" John Howard stood up in the cab of the digger with pride on his face as he looked down in the hole. "Yep! That's it!" he hollered over the roar of the running motor.

Jack Henry ran over and hooked some cables on the excavator and gave the thumbs-up.

Pastor Brown dipped his head and moved his lips in a silent prayer. Granny nudged me with her boney elbow to bow my head, and I did. Marla Maria cried out.

"Aw shut up!" Chicken Teater told her and smiled as he saw his coffin being raised from the earth. "They are going to figure out who killed me, and so help me, if it was you . . ." He shook his fist in the air in Marla Maria's direction.

Curiosity stirred in my bones. Was it going to be

easy getting Chicken Teater to the other side? Was Marla Maria Teater behind his death as Chicken believed?

She was the only one who was not only in his bed at night, but right by his deathbed, so he told me. I took my little notebook out from my back pocket. I had learned from Ruthie's investigation to never leave home without it. I jotted down what Chicken had said to Marla Maria, with prize chickens next to it, followed up by a lot of exclamation points. Oh . . . I had almost forgotten that Marla Maria was Miss Kentucky in her earlier years—a *beauty queen*—I quickly wrote that down too.

"Are you getting all of this?" Chicken questioned me and twirled his finger in a circle as he referred to the little scene Marla Maria was causing with her meltdown. She leaned her butt up against Lady Cluckington's stone. Chicken rushed over to his prize chicken's gravestone and tried to shove Marla Maria off. "Get your—"

Marla Maria jerked like she could feel something touch her. She shivered. Her body shimmied from her head to her toes.

I cleared my throat, doing my best to get Chicken to stop fusing and cursing. "Are you okay?" I asked. Did she feel him?

Granny stood there taking it all in.

Marla crossed her arms in front of her and ran her hands up and down them. "I guess when I buried Chicken, I thought that was the end of it. This is creeping me out a little bit."

End of it? End of what? Your little murder plot? My mind unleashed all sorts of ways Marla Maria might have offed her man. That seemed a little too suspicious for me. Marla buttoned her lip when Jack Henry walked over. More suspicious behavior that I duly noted.

"Can you tell me how he died?" I put a hand on her back to offer some comfort, though I knew she was putting on a good act.

She shook her head, dabbed her eye and said, "He was so sick. Coughing and hacking. I was so mad because I had bags under my eyes from him keeping me up at night." *Sniff, sniff.* "I had to dab some Preparation H underneath my eyes in order to shrink them." She tapped her face right above her cheekbones.

"That's where my butt cream went?" Chicken hooted and hollered. "She knew I had a hemorrhoid the size of a golf ball and she used my cream on her face?" Chicken flailed his arms around in the air.

I bit my lip and stepped a bit closer to Marla

Maria so I couldn't see Chicken out of my peripheral vision. There were a lot of things I had heard in my time, but hemorrhoids were something that I didn't care to know about.

I stared at Marla Maria's face. There wasn't a tear, a tear streak, or a single wrinkle on her perfectly made-up face. If hemorrhoids helped shrink her under-eye bags, did it also help shrink her wrinkles?

"Anyway, enough about me." She fanned her face with the handkerchief. "Chicken was so uncomfortable with all the phlegm. He could barely breathe. I let him rest, but called the doctor in the meantime." She nodded and waited for me to agree with her. I nodded back and she continued. "When the doctor came out of the bedroom, he told me Chicken was dead." A cry burst out of her as she threw her head back and held the hanky over her face.

I was sure she was hiding a smile from thinking she was pulling one over on me. Little did she know this wasn't my first rodeo with a murderer. Still, I patted her back while Chicken spat at her feet.

Jack Henry walked over. He didn't take his eyes off of Marla Maria.

"I'm sorry we have to do this, Marla." Jack took

his hat off out of respect for the widow. *Black widow*, I thought as I watched her fidget side to side, avoiding all eye contact by dabbing the corners of her eyes. "We are all done here, Zula." He nodded toward Granny.

Granny smiled.

Marla Maria nodded before she turned to go face her waiting public behind the police line.

Granny walked over to say something to Doc Clyde, giving him a little butt pat and making his face even redder than before. I waited until she was out of earshot before I said something to Jack Henry.

"That was weird. Marla Maria is a good actress." I made mention to Jack Henry because sometimes he was clueless as to how women react to different situations.

"Don't be going and blaming her just because she's his wife." Jack Henry was trying to play the good cop he always was, but I wasn't falling for his act. "It's all speculation at this point."

"Wife? She was no kind of wife to me." Chicken kicked his foot in the dirt John Howard had dug from his grave. "She only did one thing as my wife." Chicken looked back and watched Marla Maria play the poor pitiful widow as Beulah Paige Bellefry, president and CEO of Sleepy Hollow's gossip mill, drew her into a big hug while all the other Auxiliary women gathered to put in their two cents.

"La-la-la." I put my fingers in my ears and tried to drown him out. I only wanted to know how he was murdered, not how Marla Maria *was* a wife to him.

"She spent all my money," he cursed under his breath.

"*Shoo.*" I let out an audible sigh.

Over Jack's right shoulder, in the distance some movement caught my eye near the trailer park. There was a man peering out from behind a tree looking over at all the commotion. His John Deere hat helped shadow his face so I couldn't get a good look, but I chalked it up to being a curious neighbor like the rest of them. Still, I quickly wrote down the odd behavior. I had learned you never know what people knew. And I had to start from scratch on how to get Chicken to the great beyond. I wasn't sure, but I believe Chicken had lived in the trailer park. Maybe the person saw something, maybe not. He was going on the list.

"Are you okay?" Jack pulled off his sunglasses. His big brown eyes were set with worry. I grinned. A smile ruffled his mouth. "Just checking because of the la-la thing." He waved his hands in the air.

"I saw you taking some notes and I know what that means."

"Yep." My one word confirmed that Chicken was there and spewing all sorts of valuable information. Jack Henry was the only person who knew I was a Betweener, and he knew Chicken was right here with us even though he couldn't see him. When I told him about Chicken Teater's little visits to me and how he wouldn't leave me alone until we figured out who killed him, Jack Henry knew it to be true. "I'll tell you later."

I jotted down a note about Marla Maria spending all of Chicken's money, or so he said. Which made me question her involvement even more. Was he no use to her with a zero bank account and she offed him? I didn't know he had money.

"I can see your little noggin running a mile a minute." Jack bent down and looked at me square in the eyes.

"Just taking it all in." I bit my lip. I had learned from my last ghost that I had to keep some things to myself until I got the full scoop. And right now, Chicken hadn't given me any solid information.

"You worry about getting all the information you can from your little friend." Jack Henry pointed to the air beside me. I pointed to the air beside him where Chicken's ghost was actually standing. Jack grimaced. "Whatever. I don't care where he is." He shivered.

Even though Jack Henry knew I could see ghosts, he wasn't completely comfortable.

"You leave the investigation to me." Jack Henry put his sunglasses back on. Sexy dripped from him, making my heart jump a few beats.

"Uh-huh." I looked away. Looking away from Jack Henry when he was warning me was a common occurrence. I knew I had to do my own investigating and couldn't get lost in his eyes while lying to him.

Besides, I didn't have a whole lot of information. Chicken knew he was murdered but had no clue how. He was only able to give me clues about his life and it was up to me to put them together.

"I'm not kidding." Jack Henry took his finger and put it on my chin, pulling it toward him. He gave me a quick kiss. "We are almost finished up here. I'll sign all the paperwork and send the body on over to Eternal Slumber for Vernon to get going on some new toxicology reports we have ordered." He took his officer hat off and used his forearm to wipe the sweat off his brow.

"He's there waiting," I said. Vernon Baxter was a retired doctor who performed any and all autopsies the Sleepy Hollow police needed and I let him use Eternal Slumber for free. I had all the newest technology and equipment used in autopsies in the basement of the funeral home.

"Go on up!" Jack Henry gave John the thumbs-up and walked closer. Slowly John Howard lifted the coffin completely out of the grave and sat it right on top of the church truck, which looked like a gurney.

"Do you think she did it?" I glanced over at Marla Maria, as she talked a good talk.

"Did what?" Granny walked up and asked. She turned to see what I was looking at. "Did you dig him up because his death is being investigated for murder?" Granny gasped.

"Now Granny, don't go spreading rumors." I couldn't deny or admit to what she said. If I admitted the truth to her question, I would be betraying Jack Henry. If I denied her question, I would be lying to Granny. And no one lies to Granny.

In a lickety-split, Granny was next to her scooter.

"I'll be over. Put the coffee on," Granny hollered before she put her helmet back on her head, snapped the strap in place, and revved up the scooter and buzzed off in the direction of town, giving a little *toot-toot* and wave to the Auxiliary women as she passed.

Once the chains were unhooked from the coffin and the excavator was out of the way, Jack Henry and I guided the coffin on the church truck into the back of my hearse. Before I shut the door, I had a sick feeling that someone was watching me. Of course the crowd was still there, but I mean someone was watching *my* every move.

I looked back over my shoulder toward the trailer park. The man in the John Deere hat popped out of sight behind the tree when he saw me look at him.

I shut the hearse door and got into the driver's side. Before I left the cemetery, I looked in my rearview mirror at the tree. The man was standing there. This time the shadow of the hat didn't hide his eyes.

We locked eyes.

"Look away," Chicken Teater warned me when he appeared in the passenger seat.

Chapter 2

Chicken Teater messed with the buttons on his red plaid shirt. His black hair had always been nice and parted to the right every time I had seen him, which was often. He came around when I was younger because he was friends with my father, even though he was about ten years younger than Dad. His deep-set blue eyes showed worry.

"I guess it's time for me to get to work on trying to figure out who killed you." I gripped the steering wheel. This entire sleuthing thing was still so new I wasn't sure where to begin. But questions were what the TV mystery shows always started with. "Tell me about Lady Cluckington."

"Oh, Lady." There was pride in his voice. With

his chin in the air, he poked out his chest. "She's a feisty one. I knew she was special the first time I laid eyes on her."

"And she's a chicken?" I asked. He acted as though she was a person.

"No. That is what everyone thinks when I first talk about Lady Cluckington. She's a hen. More than a chicken. She's a beauty queen." He didn't take a breath. "She is a prize-winning hen. I only wish I was here to take care of her because I know Marla isn't. She was so jealous of Lady Cluckington."

"Do you think Marla killed you?" I knew it was a painful question, but he was the one who planted the idea in my head.

"I'd hope not, but you never know." He shook his head. "I'm just mad at her right now. After seeing her, she doesn't look like she's grieved a day for me."

"It has been almost four years," I reminded him and tried to recall how Marla Maria acted the days, weeks, even months after he was laid to rest. She still went to Girl's Best Friend Spa to get her nails and hair done on a regular basis. I had even seen her a few times at Artie's picking up some fresh cold cuts, but I never saw her truly grieving, nor did she ever thank my Granny for the beautiful service Eternal Slumber had given Chicken.

"Why was she jealous of a chicken?" It seemed odd for a beautiful woman such as Marla to be jealous of a seed-eating, beady-eyed, feathery creature.

"She's a hen. A prize hen." He took offense to calling Lady Cluckington a chicken.

"My bad." I veered the hearse around the town square, making sure I went slow. The annual Kentucky Cave Festival committee was setting up for the dance in the square to kick off a weekend of festival activities. Four years ago at the festival was the last time I had seen Chicken Teater alive. He and Marla were there. I remember because I was envious of Marla's skinny jeans and cute plaid shirt tied at the waist.

I had never been a fashion queen, and it wasn't until a few months ago that I went to Girl's Best Friend Spa and let the owner, Mary Anna Hardy, create a new style for my brown hair. Not that caramel highlights and a little layering were going to make me a beauty queen like Marla, but it did give my dull hair a little more oomph.

"What makes Lady Cluckington a prized possession?" I kept one hand on the wheel and the other twirled a strand of my hair. There was a lot of talking in the beauty chair and Marla Maria was known to flap her lips a little too much; I made a mental note to make an appointment at Girl's Best Friend Spa. Mary Anna would be more than happy to fill me in on any gossip. With the exhumation of Chicken, I was sure this was going to be headlines in the gossip circles. Everyone knew that if you wanted the latest gossip, you went to Girl's Best Friend Spa.

Marla was officially my first suspect. I read about it all the time on the Internet how the spouse was the first person questioned by the police when there was a murder investigation. If she was jealous of a hen—what would she have to gain by killing her husband? So he didn't have money. Why not divorce him? Why kill him?

"Lady is the apple of my eye." He looked over. I'd never seen a man get emotional about a chicken . . . he . . . unless he was eating it. There was a thin line of tears across his lower eyelid. "I went to the state fair when I was a boy and saw all the prize hens. I knew I had to have one, only I didn't realize how expensive the sport was."

Sport? Prize chickens were a sport? Whatever happened to the good old sports like baseball and basketball? I eyed him, but listened closely for any clues as to why Marla would have wanted him dead.

"The desire to raise a prize chicken never left my soul." He fisted his chest like Tarzan. "When I made a lot of money on a real-estate deal, I took some of my commission and bought Lady Cluckington."

Real-estate deal? As far as I knew, there hadn't been any big deals around Sleepy Hollow since all the land was locked between the caves. That was why the Inn was the only place to stay, unless you brought a tent, which many visitors did.

Plus, if he made such a big deal, why did he and Marla live in the trailer park next to the cemetery in a double wide? Surely, the beauty queen wanted something fancier.

"Oh, and I bought my Cadillac." He nodded.

"I didn't even know you had a Cadillac," I said.

Chicken Teater always drove a pickup truck so beat up that there was no way of telling what make or model it was. All I really remembered was seeing him driving around the town square in the old clunker with chicken cages stacked up in the back.

"That old beater? Nah!" He waved his hand. "I used that for me and Marla to get around in and to deliver eggs to Artie's every Saturday morning. Lady Cluckington and I took the Cadillac to the state fair every year. You know . . ." He fanned his hands in front of him. " . . . in style."

"How did Marla feel about that?" I'd put money on it that she was pissed.

"Not happy. But I was always up front with Marla before I married her about my dreams."

"What exactly was your dream?" Now Marla had motive to kill him. She took second place to a chicken. I'd imagine that wasn't a beauty queen's big accomplishment.

"To own the number-one prize hen in all of Kentucky." There was a gleam in his eye. Kind of like the one I see when a local tells me that their child was accepted into the University of Kentucky for college . . . a big feat around these parts. "Then go international and get mentioned in the *Cock and Feathers* magazine."

"*Cock and Feathers*?" Good golly, was there really a magazine dedicated to the fowls?

"It's an international magazine for prize hens," his voice trailed off as though he realized his dream had never come true.

"I'm sorry." There wasn't much more I could say to make him feel better. Not only had his dreams not come true, he was also murdered. Poor guy couldn't get a break.

We pulled into Eternal Slumber. There was a news crew there from Lexington.

"Un-holy hell." Chicken craned his neck to see all the commotion. "The festival is really getting some good coverage."

In my rearview mirror, I saw the anchorman for the five o'clock news rushing up behind the hearse.

"I have a sneaky suspicion they aren't here for the festival." I took a deep breath and opened the door.

"Ms. Raines," the man stuck the microphone in my face. "Can you tell us why the Sleepy Hollow police exhumed the body of Colonel C. Teater?"

"No comment." I darted to the back of the hearse. I felt like a celebrity. A local one at least.

"Is it true they have reopened his death case and changed it to homicide?" The man threw questions at me left and right.

Whoop, whoop. Sirens blared behind me, causing me to look. Jack Henry jumped out of his police car and put his hands out.

"Okay, give Ms. Raines some room." He backed up the reporter away from me. Luckily, the reporter started to drill Jack with all sorts of questions, but Jack was truly tight-lipped about the whole thing.

"If only they could see me." Chicken stood next to the camera and put his face in the lens. "Hello!" He waved, hoping to get his five minutes of fame. Unfortunately, his five minutes looked like it was going to be more like national coverage. . . . If only it wasn't because he was murdered.

Chapter 3

That was crazy," I said to Jack Henry. My heart was pounding a mile a minute. I glanced out the front door of the funeral home.

News about Chicken Teater's exhumation was spreading like wildfire. Two more news crews showed up before we could get the church truck safely into the funeral home. Jack had a heck of a time fending off the camera crews. They were positioned on the sidewalk in front of Eternal Slumber and across the street in the square.

"I wonder how they found out about the exhumation." Jack peeled back the curtain on the front door and looked out.

"Oh I don't know." Sarcasm dripped from my lips. "Duh. The entire town came out to see what was going on. I'm sure one of them tipped off the news." I signed off on the papers and handed them to Vernon, who was waiting near the elevator to take Chicken to the basement, where he could begin his work on the remains.

Jack just looked at me. I crinkled my nose and smiled. He smiled back, causing my heart to flutter. If he didn't stop making cute faces at me, they were going to have to make a spot on the church truck next to Chicken, because I swore my heart stopped every time Jack looked at me.

"This should be fun." Vernon took the papers and slapped them on top of the dirty casket before wheeling the church truck into the open elevator.

"Remember, this is a closed investigation," Jack Henry warned Vernon. "No talking to the media or friends or family about this."

"Scout's honor." Vernon put up two fingers before the elevator door shut.

"Dinner tonight?" Jack Henry asked.

"Dinner? How about breakfast, so I can tell you what I know about Chicken and who I think might have done it?" There was still an assumption on my part that I would play some sort of roll in the investigation of the death, even though he had already told me to stay out of it.

"Emma Lee, you know I believe you see

Chicken, just like you saw Ruthie." He rubbed his hand over my cheek, leaving me momentarily paralyzed. "But you said Chicken didn't know how he was murdered, which means you need to leave it up to the professionals. I've already warned you. I can't have you getting involved in something that could possibly put you in danger. I couldn't live with myself if that happened."

I nodded. For a moment, I lost all my marbles and all cohesive thoughts melted away.

"What?" Chicken jumped out of the curtains. "You tell that little whippersnapper that I was murdered and he needs to check Marla out. She was so jealous of Lady Cluckington. She signed the agreement! You have to find the agreement, Emma Lee."

What agreement? If he and Marla had an agreement, it was news to me.

Agreement or not, Jack Henry wasn't going to let me get my hands dirty.

"But he's my client." I protested and kept the little information about Chicken and Marla's agreement to myself. This agreement might be the first bit of information that would help lead to more clues. And completely pin Marla Maria as the number-one suspect, which she already was in my book.

"Four years ago he was Eternal Slumber's client." He put his hat on, a sure sign he was leaving. "Today he is *my* client." His expression grew serious.

"But he's here." I pointed to Chicken standing right next to Jack Henry. I smiled, trying to break his icy look. "Doesn't that mean something?"

Jack Henry looked to his right and did a little shimmy shake. "Don't do that to me, Emma Lee." He shook his arms and hands like he was shaking off the dead. "You know I can't stand to know there is a ghost next to me. It creeps me out."

"Fine, but he *is* my client," I noted. "From the afterworld."

"What?" Jack cocked his eyebrow. "You have a business going with them now?"

"No, but that's a good idea." *Hell no*, I wanted to shout. There would be no other ghosts after Chicken. Even though the psychic said, once a Betweener, always a Betweener. She also said it was probably limited to people I knew and there weren't too many people I had buried that I knew. Especially those who had been murdered.

Granted, I never thought Chicken Teater was murdered, nor Ruthie, but Ruthie proved otherwise and I guessed Chicken was trying to do the same.

"Dinner?" Jack walked back over and grabbed both of my hands before he pulled them up to his lips and gently kissed them.

My heart skipped a beat. Jack Henry was a dream come true. When I was in high school, I would have done anything to catch his eye. But no one really wanted anything to do with the creepy funeral-home girl. Or so I thought.

"That was something to see." Granny walked into the vestibule. She must have let herself in the back door. "I've never seen that in all the years I'd been in the business." She walked over to the curtain and peeled it back; then yanked it again to open it wide.

The sounds of clicks could be heard from the outside, as Granny stood smiling and waving to the media from the vestibule window. Chicken was right behind her doing the same thing.

"It's something we try not to do often." Jack Henry let go of my hands and walked over to shut the curtain. Granny waved until it was closed. He didn't scold her. He knew better. Granny did what Granny wanted to do. Apparently, Chicken did too.

"Dinner, Emma Lee?" He asked again—this time wanting a definite answer. "What do you say I take you to Bella Vino?"

"What time?" *No-brainer.* I could already taste the delicious chicken parmesan from my favorite restaurant . . . *our restaurant.* I ignored Granny, who was still trying to sneak a peek at the media. I had to admit, this was the only time Sleepy Hollow had seen so much press.

"Seven." He bent down and kissed me on the cheek before he left out the door to the waiting camera crew.

"True love." Granny giggled. Over her shoulder, I snuck a peek out the window where the cameramen were trying to coerce Jack into talking. They had no clue he was as ironclad as they come.

"He is a keeper," I said to Granny. "You *have* to be careful on that scooter. You are going to kill someone."

I walked back through the family gathering space that was next to the kitchen to start the coffee Granny had told me to brew.

"So." Granny rubbed her hands together. "What exactly is going on? I know you had to have a good reason to dig him up. Murder? Someone steal something out of his coffin? I've heard of grave robbers." A devilish look came into her eyes. "Who's the suspect?"

Although it sounded really sick, there were people out there who stole items off the dead.

I couldn't even think of that, in fear of being haunted all my life. That thought scared me.

"Granny, you know I can't mix business with pleasure." I ignored her beady little eyes staring at me.

"Need I remind you that I still own this establishment and have the right to kick you out of it?"

"You wouldn't." I gasped, and stared at her in disbelief.

"Then tell me what is going on." She straightened up and spoke in a pretty little Southern tone.

"Granny, I have Southern charm just like you, lest you forget that you taught me." *Please hurry up and brew,* I thought, looking at the coffee. The quicker she got her cup of coffee, the quicker she'd be out of here. "And you can't keep holding it over my head that you own the joint. We have a contract—signed papers."

"Oh, I forgot about that." Her mouth twitched to the side. "Well I'm just curious. I won't tell anyone. Besides, what good is it that you are dating the sheriff if we don't get the scoop?"

She did have a point. Still. I couldn't betray Jack Henry and his trust.

"I'm telling you right now that I'm going to have the papers drawn up and you can sell the place to Charlotte and me." My eyes narrowed. Granny and I both knew it was time to sell the place. She hadn't had her hand in any part of the business since Charlotte and I took over.

"So you aren't going to tell me?" There was no doubt Granny was persistent.

"No," my voice was thick and unsteady because I was itching to tell her.

"Fine." Granny took a deep breath and pulled her shoulders back. "Now, tell me." There was a spark of interest in her eyes.

Without telling her a word, I handed her the papers Jack Henry had given me with the warrant.

"What kind of evidence do they have?" Granny's mouth formed an *O*. There was no way to hide the surprised expression on Granny's face. "Marla Maria?"

"Don't go pointing fingers." I grabbed the pot of coffee and poured each of us a cup. "Jack Henry isn't going to tell me what evidence he has." Which wasn't a lie. He didn't have any evidence except Chicken's ghost and me. Thank goodness, Jack Henry was in charge. This type of evidence to exhume a body would have never gone this easily in a big town. "And we don't know if Marla Maria had anything to do with it. She did look sad today."

"Sad my patookie." Granny sipped her coffee as she referred to her behind. The steam swirled up around her face and clouded over her eyes. Without seeing Granny's expression, she knew as much as I did that Marla Maria was a great actress.

Chapter 4

Across the street from Eternal Slumber Funeral Home was the town square, where the annual Kentucky Cave Festival mainly took place, as it should, since it was in the middle of the town with all the main streets leading away from it. The festival had been going on for a couple hundred years. In fact, the city records show in one way or another, the celebration of the caves had started from the first time many of them were discovered.

Granted, they probably didn't celebrate like we do today. It was important for the festival to be successful in today's down economy. The festival committee got smart and decided to capitalize on the seasonal change of the caves—the spring and fall. Therefore, every spring and every fall Sleepy

Hollow was the host to the largest festival in Kentucky.

This one happened to be my favorite. The flowers this time of the year were amazing and the spring foliage in the caves were nothing short of magic. The colors popped in the dark caverns, dimly lit by the visitors' torches used on tours. A few years back, the committee hosted a fundraiser in order to put limited electricity in the caves for those "just in case" moments. The ones we didn't like to think of. Like falling down the cave and landing on a stalagmite. One would think that would hurt—being stabbed by a collection of cave droppings that formed a sharp pointy cone. The thought of it sent the willies up my legs.

"Mornin' Emma Lee! Mornin' Zula Fae!" Hettie Bell shouted from the top of the ladder on the gazebo steps, steadying the wobbling rickety old wooden thing while hanging on to the lattice around the old structure with one hand and waving with the other. "Lots of stuff happening today!"

Normally I'd yell back; instead, I bid Granny good-bye and decided to walk over since the camera crew was still camped out in front of Eternal Slumber, and all the reporters had their microphones at their hips as if there was a gun-slinging about to happen between my lips. I pinched them together to make sure not even a bit of air escaped them.

Granny jumped on her moped and zoomed across the square toward the Inn, but not before giving a big ol' wave and "hi y'all" to the cameras.

The festival committee was busy draping the small white festival lanterns all over the trees while some food RVs had set up along the perimeter, and there was poor Hettie Bell hanging on for dear life.

"She's going to kill someone if she doesn't slow that thing down." Hettie shook her head as we watched Granny swerve a little too far left, almost running into a park bench.

"You tell her that." I shuddered inwardly at the thought of the tongue-lashing Granny would give Hettie Bell if she tried to tell Granny how to ride the scooter. "Let me help." I held on to both sides of the ladder, bearing all the weight I could so she could finish stringing the lights. "Everyone seems to be excited."

"That's an understatement." Hettie draped the end of the cord around a hole in the lattice and plugged it into the end of another set of lights. "I hope it brings in a crowd for the festival."

"I was talking about the festival." The roar of

the generators from the roach-coaches hummed along with all the birds singing throughout the square.

"I'm talking about the body you exhumed. You interrupted morning yoga." She climbed down and smoothed out her very chic chin-length bob. Her black eyes bore into mine for the big dark secret. "What was up with that?"

"I just do what the police warrant tells me to do. I'm sorry I ruined your class." I knew she meant that she didn't get paid since everyone was at the cemetery.

"I was doing my morning yoga class on the front porch of the Inn. You should have seen them. Zula Fae included." A grin crossed her lips, exposing beautiful white teeth. "I swear they heard the click of the tractor key before John Howard turned it. They bolted to the edge of the veranda and once they heard the hum of the tractor, they ran across the square faster than jackrabbits. Zula Fae was beside herself looking for her moped key, cursing and throwing things out of drawers trying to find the extra set. Once she found them, she jumped on the moped, gunning it as fast as it would go."

"Yep, she's going to kill someone with that thing." I shook my head.

It wasn't like Hettie and I were big buds. She recently moved to Whispering Falls and started the new yoga studio, Pose and Relax. She bought the abandoned building next to Eternal Slumber, which she was renovating. Until the new space was finished, she was holding her classes at the Sleepy Hollow Inn, where Granny's customers loved to wake up to a good morning stretch. Plus all the Auxiliary women went, not only to gossip, but because Doc Clyde had told them it would be good for their joints. I had thought about going because I heard flexibility was good for the bedroom—not that Jack Henry and I had slept together, though the thought wasn't far from my mind.

Still, I could do yoga for the just-in-case-it-did-happen factor. And I would get to see my granny.

"I'm headed down for my shift at the Inn." Hettie pointed across the square in the direction of Granny's place. Hettie worked at the Inn part-time, helping Granny clean rooms, do dishes, or even cook. The Inn was packed for the Kentucky Cave Festival. Until recently, it was the only place to stay near the square; now there was a big hotel on the outskirts of town. Still, visitors loved the charm of the old Inn and Granny always provided plenty of entertainment—herself. "I have to do the morning-rush dishes. I told her I'd be there right after I did my committee duty of stringing the lights on the gazebo. My work here is done. Want to come?" She dusted her hands off and folded up the ladder. She propped it up on the gazebo and motioned for someone to come get it.

"I can't." I pointed toward the front of the square. "I've got some business to take care of at the courthouse. But I'll see you tomorrow morning for yoga and plenty of times during the festival."

We parted ways. Off in the distance I could see Cheryl Lynne Doyle setting up her little roach-coach stand for Higher Grounds Café. Another good cup of coffee might just be what I needed to get me through the day.

"You have this city all in an uproar and here we are trying to get this festival ready for tomorrow night," she said in her slow Southern drawl and smoothed the edges of the awning dangling from her childhood RV.

Food vendors from all over Kentucky set up small booths or RVs along the perimeter of the town square so the festival-goers could sample their food. For a price of course.

"I had nothing to do with it." I put my hands in the air before I gestured toward the coffee carafe setup. "I do what I'm told."

"Yeah, fix yourself a cup. It's still fresh. I brought

it over from the shop so I could drink some while I got ready for tomorrow." Cheryl Lynne and I grew up together in Sleepy Hollow. It wasn't until high school that Cheryl Lynne blossomed and suddenly got very popular, leaving me in the dust, and I don't mean cremation dust . . . social dust.

Cheryl Lynne had gone on a senior trip to New York City, and when she discovered the fancy coffee houses she knew that a coffee shop was exactly what Sleepy Hollow needed. And with the Doyle money, her daddy had no problem buying up the old post-office building next to the courthouse to give Cheryl Lynne her own coffee house, Higher Grounds Café.

The Sleepy Hollow Barbershop Quartet had taken residence in the gazebo with their pitch pipes, snapping fingers, and foot tapping as they tried to figure out the acoustics to make their music soar like the birds around Sleepy Hollow.

They would be at the opening ceremony and the Cattlemen's Association cookout tonight. Too bad I was going to miss it, which I didn't mind because my night was going to be spent looking deep into Jack Henry's eyes over candlelight, pasta, and a few glasses of wine at Bella Vino. That beats a hamburger and a four-man quartet any day.

The caves were a draw for many musicians. The sounds of guitars, singers, and makeshift drums could be heard in the late hours of any given night from the hollows of the nooks and crannies between the caves and in the gorges surrounding Sleepy Hollow. Local gossip had it that bluegrass music was discovered right here. But we all knew where local gossip got us.

Speaking of local gossip, five-foot-six Beulah Paige Bellefry trotted toward Cheryl Lynne like a show pony in her six-inch heels, tight two-piece baby-blue pantsuit, pearls cascading down around her neck, and her storebought eyelashes batting against her fake-and-bake tanned face.

She snapped her neck to the sounds of the quartet and waved her hand in the air. "Emma, Emma Lee Raines." Now her shoulders wiggled to the beat of the hand claps coming from the four-man band.

"Good grief," Cheryl Lynne turned away from Beulah. "We haven't even had our coffee yet."

"Good morning, ladies." Beulah meant one lady. Me. She had her back to Cheryl. "Tell me what is going on with Eternal Slumber. I have to know."

"I'm sorry Beulah, what do you mean?" I always tried to be nice to her, but it was very difficult. Granny always told me to kill them with kindness, which proved hard to do when Beulah had no remorse for the rumors she started.

"I heard everyone is digging up their loved ones and demanding to transfer them to Burns Funeral Home." There wasn't a sympathetic tone in her voice. In fact, I did believe there was a twinkle in her blues eyes that lingered a little too long on me.

O'Dell Burns, owner of Burns Funeral Home, was Eternal Slumber's only competition in the area and was always trying to steal our clients from us. The funeral business can be very tricky. It was more than putting on a pretty service; it was about building a relationship with the family to help ensure future business. No matter what the economy did, there was always going to be need for a funeral home and it was my job to make sure the services went well, but it was Charlotte Rae's job to keep the business coming.

"Who told you something as ridiculous as that?" I quipped. To Cheryl I said, "Who would say something so stupid?" Then I gave a sideways glance toward Beulah Paige with a cocked brow.

Anger boiled in me. That was an O'Dell Burns move if I had ever seen one. He would stop at nothing to get the clients we had. He knew if he told Beulah, it would spread like wildfire.

"You better watch her, Emma Lee." Chicken scowled inches away from Beulah Paige. He referred to her gossiping and loose tongue. "She could lick a skillet that was in the kitchen from the front porch."

A noisy burst of coffee shot out of my mouth. I tried to contain the spew, but Chicken had tickled my funny bone and I couldn't stop myself.

"Are you okay?" Cheryl asked.

I waved her off and tried to compose myself.

In one fell swoop, Beulah stood with her legs wide apart, the hems of her pants tugged too tight, put her hands on her hips and then plunged her body forward; she moved her hands, letting them rest on the ground while lifting her head, and looked right past me, staring straight ahead.

"Have you gone mad, Beulah?" Cheryl's face contorted. Beulah was a sight to behold with her butt stuck up in the air right here in the town square for all to see. "Everyone in this town has gone crazy."

"Emma Lee is stressing me out. I have to get to the bottom of why they dug up Chicken Teater after four years of undisturbed rest." Beulah closed her eyes and took a deep breath and did the sign of the cross. "This is the Prasarita Padottanasana pose that Hettie Bell told me to do when I begin to feel stress creeping in my shoulders. And Emma Lee is making me stressed."

"You are the one who came over to me." I jabbed my finger in her turned-up-nosed face. "You are the one stressing me out with all this talk about people wanting to take their business away from me. Shame on you, Beulah Paige Bellefry!" I stomped off in the direction of the courthouse.

"Can you help me up?" I heard Beulah Paige ask Cheryl Lynn for some assistance. There was no way I was going to turn around to see what a fool she had made of herself.

I did wish I could tell everyone why Jack Henry ordered the exhumation of Chicken Teater. I wished I could tell everyone I was a Betweener medium and that their loved ones were okay. But I couldn't. In fact, when I got knocked out by that perilous plastic Santa, I told Charlotte Rae and Granny I had seen Chicken at my bedside. It gave them all sorts of fits, thinking I was as crazy as a june bug. After Doc Clyde diagnosed me with the "Funeral Trauma," they were a bit more forgiving. Granny always warned me to hide my crazy. Only hiding crazy would mean I'd have to hide my whole life. The entire bunch of us are loons.

I took meds and did the therapist route which

was what Doc Clyde told me to do, but no matter how much I tried to ignore the ghosts, they never went away until I figured out who murdered them.

Jack Henry was right. If anyone found out we had exhumed Chicken because we *thought*, with good reason, he might have been murdered, Sleepy Hollow residents would go crazy rushing to the store to pick up a gun and some shells. Not to mention, if word got around that Sleepy Hollow was unsafe to visit, our economy would take a dive. Especially now since the Kentucky Cave Festival was our biggest economy boost.

Still, I wanted to give Beulah Paige Bellefry and her yoga moves a piece of my mind.

Chapter 5

My feet pounded as I trudged up the courthouse steps. Beulah Paige always knew how to punch the right buttons with me. I was going to get my frustration out in one form or the other. Once I had publicly threatened her and it came back to bite me in the butt when she ended up in a coma, making me look like I had tried to "off" her when it wasn't true. Luckily, Jack Henry came to my rescue and did all the undercover work proving my innocence. Now I'm careful about the things I say to people, especially in public, because you never know who is around and who will use it against you.

"Good morning." I greeted some people standing in the hallway of the courthouse waiting for the nine-o'clock opening time with a smile and a nod. The chimes on the courthouse clock dinged, letting us all know it was time. "Just in time." I shrugged and made my way to the records room.

Chicken said there was an agreement between him and Marla Maria. His will would be filed at the courthouse and open for public viewing. I was sure he had a will if Marla Maria was taking care of Lady Cluckington. Which reminded me that I needed to make a visit to Marla Maria's and get a good look at the prize hen. I chuckled at the thought of the two *queens* going after each other.

"Oh." The deputy clerk eyed me from behind the records counter. "You're back."

"I am." The last time I was here had to do with Ruthie's death and I had the poor clerk going through dozens of files to find what I needed. Hey, that was her job. "I'm looking for the will of Colonel C. Teater."

The deputy slid the old steel ladder that rolled along the walls of the records room to the *T*'s and she climbed up in record time and retrieved Chicken's file.

She slapped the thick file on the counter. "Let me know if you need something copied."

"Will do." I smiled and turned my attention to the file. There were public documents in there, like his record of taxes, marriage, and other things that held no merit. One thing did catch my eye. A tax document for a piece of real estate he had mentioned earlier. My jaw dropped when my eyes found the taxable value. The property was valued at a half million dollars. Not a bad little payday if he did sell it. I wondered if Marla Maria knew about it. Unfortunately, there wasn't a will or a reference to an attorney to tell me anything about an agreement.

I took out my notebook and jotted down some information about the property. I flipped through more of the pages to see if there happened to be another bill of sale, but there wasn't anything there.

"Excuse me." I pushed the paper to the edge of the counter. The deputy walked back over, not without sighing. "Can you see if this has been sold or if Mr. Colonel C. Teater still owns the property?"

She took the paper without acknowledgement. There was no reason to be so testy; after all, it was her job. She'd thank me later when the killer was brought to justice, making her safe and sound in our little town. While she was gone, I rummaged through the papers again and snapped pictures of them with my cell. I wasn't going to waste any more time having the deputy make me some copies. *Gotta love cell phones.*

"Nope." She sauntered back into the room like she was on a Sunday drive. "He still owns it." She walked away.

Technically, he didn't own it because he was dead. Whoever was in the will owned it. But who was that? I stood there for a moment staring blankly at Chicken's public records trying to decide if this was enough information for Jack Henry. *Nah.* I had to find out for myself. I had to find that agreement.

"Thank you!" I hollered to the deputy, who was helping someone else, and shoved the file to the edge of the counter to let her know I was done.

The same people were in the hall when I walked out of the records room. Granny was also there.

"What's going on?" I moseyed up to her. "I thought you were busy at the Inn."

"I am. Hettie Bell came over after she finished decorating the square and is lookin' after the place for me." Granny rolled up on her toes to see over the people in front of her. "I have to get my name on the ballot and get back in time for yoga since your little exhumation of Chicken took our yoga time."

"Ballot?" Many things Granny said hit a nerve,

making me pause. The first was *ballot*. What ballot did she want her name on? And yoga?

"I've decided to run for mayor." A glint in Granny's eyes told me she was serious.

"What?" Shock and awe took over. My mouth dropped. Granny wasn't old, but was she already going senile?

"I was thinking . . ." She bit her lip. Oh, I didn't want her to think too hard, that always got us in trouble. "Since we are in-between mayors and I have lived here all my life and have owned two businesses, I think I know what this town needs."

"What would that be?" I put my hands on my hips and prepared myself for the response she was about to give.

"A little dose of Zula Fae Raines Payne. That is what this town needs! Vote Zula!" She pumped her fist in the air. A few people cheered her on. "See?" She gestured toward the line of people.

"I think this town has gone mad," I leaned over and whispered into Granny's ear. "Have you had your head checked? You need your boyfriend to give you a full physical."

"I will do no such thing. I'm a Southern lady." Granny stretched her arms out to the side, and swinging them in an upward motion, she placed them palm to palm and brought them back down in front of her chest. "Ohmmm . . ." she hummed.

"What are you doing?" Embarrassment crept up my neck and settled on my cheeks. She was old but she wasn't old enough to lose her ever-loving mind. "Maybe you have the Funeral Trauma."

"Shh." Granny closed her eyes. "You are knocking my balance off. Hettie Bell said this was a good exercise for my mojo."

"Mojo?" I rolled my eyes. "You don't need mojo, you need some common sense."

"Zula Fae Raines Payne?" The clerk hollered out into the crowd. "You're up!"

"Oh," Granny pushed me aside, "I've got to run. Toodle-oo!" Granny put her hand in the air and gave me the spirit-finger good-bye gesture.

Hettie Bell was making all the old women in the community nuts with all this relaxation deep-breathing bull crap. Granny was in no mood to hear any sort of reasoning of why she shouldn't run for mayor and I certainly wasn't going to waste my breath or time. Right now, my time was more valuably spent trying to figure out who killed Chicken Teater and trying to get him to the other side.

Chapter 6

Not long after I had left the courthouse I made it back to Eternal Slumber and noticed Charlotte Rae's car in the parking lot. I marched myself right into the funeral home and straight into her office.

"Charlotte Rae." I pushed open the door. She sat in her chair, her long red hair falling around her face and cascading down each shoulder. Her natural beauty was plagued with worry wrinkles and the look in her eyes suddenly made me feel queasy.

"Emma Lee, Granny has done it again." She shook her head. "It's not the fact I'm getting a gazillion calls from clients who are worried we are going to dig their loved ones up—which was

your fault—but now she's running for mayor."
Charlotte threw her hands in the air. "If she
doesn't win over O'Dell Burns, we are going to be
losing every single family on our client list."

"O'Dell Burns?" I asked.

"That is who she is running against." Her spar-
kly green eyes had lost a tad tiny bit of their natural sparkle.

"That is why she's running." *Sneaky Granny.* My
eyelids lowered and I scowled. "Sneaky Granny.
Very sneaky."

How did I not figure out that Granny had
an ulterior motive? She always had an ulterior
motive. The only reason she gave control of Eternal Slumber to Charlotte Rae and me was because
she married Earl Way Payne, who was divorced
from Granny's archnemesis, Ruthie Sue—my first
ghost, who had been sure Granny was the one
who killed her. Ruthie and Earl had owned the
Sleepy Hollow Inn together.

Five years ago, Earl Way Payne died while still
married to Granny. On the day of his funeral, Earl
Way's will was read, leaving Granny his half of
the Inn.

So while he had updated his will, Earl Way
hadn't changed his "pre-need" funeral arrangements when he married my granny and hadn't

let her know what his plans were. So, Granny had Earl Way laid out as if he were the king of England with a room full of Sleepy Hollow residents paying their respects when O'Dell Burns marched in rolling a casket cot with Ruthie right behind him. Little did we know that before Earl and Granny wed, he had made arrangements at Burns Funeral Home.

"Pick him up," Ruthie had demanded, pointing back and forth from Earl Way's body to the basic wooden box O'Dell had wheeled in. "Go on, put him in."

I had never seen Granny rendered speechless, but she was that day. O'Dell picked up Earl Way's body and plopped him right in that cheap pine box.

Granny stood at the front door of Eternal Slumber with her arms crossed as O'Dell barreled out of the viewing room with Earl bouncing and Ruthie scurrying alongside.

As a result of Earl's estate plan, Ruthie Sue and Granny became co-owners of the Inn, and Granny moved in right away, making sure Ruthie Sue had to look at her on a daily basis. And she will never forgive O'Dell Burns for the low-down dirty stunt he pulled.

"Emma Lee, are you listening to me?" Charlotte's fiery redheaded temper was flaring up. "You are the one who is close to her. You have *got* to knock some sense into her."

"What do you expect me to do? She's a grown woman." Granny would knock me into next Sunday if I told her not to do something. *"It's Granny!"* I reminded her of how persnickety Granny was and could be.

"And she's lost her mind." Charlotte burst out in tears. "She's going to run Eternal Slumber into the ground."

Charlotte Rae punched away on a calculator.

Numbers. Numbers. Numbers. Who cared about all the numbers?

"The death business isn't about numbers. It's about being personal and empathizing with the family. Granny is good at that." I reminded her of why everyone in Sleepy Hollow wanted to bring their loved ones to us. "Maybe she'd be a good mayor."

Who was I kidding? I didn't want Granny being mayor any more than Charlotte Rae did.

"I've got it!" Charlotte Rae jumped up and rushed around the desk. "I'm going to do a press release about the exhumation and work with a public relations firm out of Lexington, because this alone is what O'Dell is going to try to use in his campaign against Granny. Plus, we don't need the bad press. Especially after we have recovered from charges against Granny for killing Ruthie Sue."

When I didn't say anything, Charlotte looked up at me.

"Well? Don't you have something to do? Like go see Granny and stop her from this nonsense?" Charlotte shooed me out the door before I could put in my two cents' worth. She obviously hadn't heard a word I said. And they were good words too.

"I'll add it to the list," I grumbled under my breath. The list was getting fairly long. I needed to go see Marla Maria and Lady Cluckington before I could even bring myself to think about Granny. She had obviously lost her marbles, or else that yoga stuff was opening up brain cells that were meant to stay closed.

"It better be at the top!" Charlotte slammed the door behind me.

My office was a couple of doors down from Charlotte's, but I could still hear her smacking things on her desk and yelling out profanities about Granny's behavior. I was in no mood to hear her rant and rave. I grabbed the hearse keys and my purse. It was time for me to drive to the hood—the trailer hood.

"Keep two hands on the wheel." Chicken Teater appeared in the back of the hearse, lying down where a casket would be with his arms crossed over his chest.

"Are you a vampire ghost now?" I glanced in the rearview mirror.

"Ruthie Sue didn't tell me you were a jokester. Though she did mention you were a little scatter-brained and blamed it on the Santa incident." The next thing I knew, Chicken was in the front passenger seat next to me. I mean really close to me. His left arm draped around my neck and rested on my shoulder.

"Do you mind?" I shrugged.

"Two hands." He didn't scoot over. He pointed straight ahead. "Eyes on the road."

"How can I drive safely with you right next to me? Do you think you can die . . . twice?" I asked with a smart-alecky tone.

"Ruthie also forgot to mention how cute you are." He didn't budge. "Charlotte Rae has always taken the beauty limelight; but you, Emma Lee, you are a beauty in your own right."

"What does that mean? Do you think I would take your compliment seriously?" I didn't put much weight on his observation. "You think a chicken is the most beautiful thing."

"Wait until you see Lady Cluckington." Pride dripped on his face. "You are going to be jealous of her just like Marla Maria is."

"Speaking of Marla Maria." It was time to ask Chicken about the agreement he spoke about before he disappeared on me. I might be a Betweener, but I had no way of telling him I might need to talk to him when he wasn't around. I had to get all my questions answered while he was right here. "I went to the courthouse to see if you had a will."

"Why would you do that?" Chicken acted as if I had two heads.

"Because most people have to leave their things to someone, and you wouldn't leave Lady Cluckington to just *anyone*." Out of the corner of my eye, I could see Chicken was studying every word I was saying. I had his attention. "What was in the agreement between you and Marla Maria?"

"She signed it. It's in the house." Chicken nodded enthusiastically. "Lady Cluckington is worth a lot of money if she continues to win in shows."

"What was the agreement?" I needed details of the terms.

"Marla Maria, though she never told me, was envious of my and Lady's relationship." He took his arm from around my shoulder and crossed them in front of him. "I have a little bit of money and only a very good friend of mine knows where it is. Marla Maria has to take care of Lady until she comes with me to the great beyond."

"Take care, as in how?" I asked.

Chicken pointed for me to turn into the trailer park. He was an Eternal Slumber client, but I didn't go to clients' houses.

"She has to clean her cage, keep her bathed, feed her the right foods, and enter her into contests. You know—continue everything I wanted to do with Lady." He pointed again. I turned the car down another street. "What the hell? What is she doing in my and Lady Cluckington's Cadillac? She knows she can't ride in the caddy unless it's official business."

Marla Maria was getting in the driver's side of the Cadillac. She had on a too-tight black sweater that clung perfectly to her curves and stopped just shy of the top of her skintight black leggings, showing off a little skin in between. The five-inch black stiletto heels made her already slender legs even longer and thinner. Her hair was pinned up with a red bandana neatly tied around her neck, making her red lipstick stand out even more. Way more.

If she had a nickel in her back pocket, I could tell if it was heads or tails.

"That outfit is a far cry from what she had on this morning." I pulled up in front of a double-wide trailer a couple of trailers down from his double-wide. There was a tree with all sorts of empty wine bottles hanging from the branches that were, hopefully, keeping the hearse out of sight. It was hard not to notice a hearse, and Marla Maria would know it was mine. After all, ETERNAL SLUMBER was printed on each side.

Chicken's small grassy yard was filled with chicken and hen lawn ornaments. The wind chime was dangling hens. Marla Maria stood with her back to us.

No wonder she killed you. Who would want to ride in a beat up truck when you owned a Cadillac? The words almost escaped my mouth, but I knew I'd be better off keeping my lips shut.

"Marla Maria, baby!" A man yelled from across the gravel road. He looked both ways before he crossed. I squinted trying to get a good look at his face. Unfortunately, his John Deere hat shadowed his face down to his chin.

"Baby?" Chicken fussed. "Well. That no good sonofabitch! I'm gonna jerk a knot in your ass!"

Before I could say anything, Chicken was out

of the hearse and right next to Marla Maria baby, winding up his arm to get a good swing at the guy in the John Deere hat. Not paying a bit of attention to Chicken and his tomfoolery, I rolled down my window to see if I could hear what Marla Maria baby was saying to the guy.

"I'll show you *baby*!" Chicken swung. His fist went right through the guy's jaw. For a brief second Marla and the guy's conversation came to a halt. The man took his hat off and rubbed his jaw. He was much younger than Chicken, I'd guess by ten or fifteen years. He wasn't a native to the area or I would have known him. He had deep blue eyes, a five-o'clock shadow, and appeared to be muscular under his green Henley shirt. Not half bad looking. Especially standing next to Chicken, whose hair was now falling down in his face.

"I think I just got a toothache." John Deere hat guy thrust his jaw side-to-side and front to back. He opened his mouth and Marla Maria looked in.

"I think he felt my fist!" Chicken hollered over to me. The couple said a few words, but I couldn't hear them because Chicken continued dancing around telling the guy he was going to give it to him some more and continued to wind up his arm, laying a few more air punches on the guy's jaw.

"Come on, Duckie." Marla Maria rolled her eyes before she walked over to the passenger side of the Cadillac. He did what he was told.

"Duckie?" Chicken fisted his hand and punched the palm of the other like he was going to sock Duckie again. "What is it with Marla Maria and fowl names?"

I couldn't help but laugh. He did have a point.

Marla and the Duckie jumped into the Caddy. I slithered down in the seat so they didn't see me— even though the hearse was a good indication that I was there. The car sped by so fast they probably didn't pay any attention to me.

"What are you waiting for?" Chicken appeared right next to me in the passenger seat, sucking up the air around me. He jutted his finger in the air. "Follow my Cadillac!"

"I'm not following anyone." I reversed the hearse and eased up to Chicken's double-wide.

"What kind of detective are you?" Chicken silently fumed with his arms crossed over his chest.

"I never said I was a detective. I'm a funeral-home director," I reminded him. "You have to remember you are the second ghost I have ever helped. I still don't know what I'm doing."

"How come Ruthie Sue Payne raved on about how good you are?"

"If you don't like what I'm doing, I will be more than happy to bury your ungrateful murdered butt six feet under and forget all about our little visits." My blood pressure rose and I swallowed hard to get my wits about me. I could threaten him all I wanted to, but I knew he wasn't going to leave me alone until I figured out who killed him. I put the car back in reverse like I was going to leave the trailer park.

"Wait . . . wait." Chicken put his hands out in front of him. "It's hard seeing my Marla Maria dating another man."

"How do you know she's dating another man?"

"He called her baby. And no man calls a woman baby without more intentions." Chicken had a point. The guy did have a tone about his voice. "And he's wanted my Marla since we moved to the trailer park."

"Did Marla ever give him the time of day?" This was probably a hard question for Chicken to answer. It would be an important piece of the pie.

"She never had the chance to. I ran him off every single time." Chicken snorted. "One time I had Lady Cluckington chase him clear across the trailer park. He looked like a fool running as fast as his scrawny legs could carry him."

"Looks like we have company." I watched a dark Ford sedan pull up behind us.

"Aw shucks." A big smile crossed Chicken's lips. "That's my buddy, Sugar."

"Sugar?" What the hell had I gotten myself into? Who has the name Chicken? Who has the name Sugar?

"Sprinkle a little Sugar on it." Chicken broke out into a fit of laughter. "That's what he used to say to all the girls down at the Watering Hole to get a date. They all flocked over to him. That's where I met my Marla Maria."

Hmm. I wondered what type of women went to the Watering Hole Bar. My parents forbade me to go there and now that they've retired to Florida, I might just have to stop by.

Sugar stepped out of his sedan. All five feet of him. He dabbed his hairline with his handkerchief and replaced it in the pocket of his blue jeans.

"He has always been such a snappy dresser." Chicken slapped his hands together in delight when the spurs on Sugar's cowboy boots jingled as Sugar walked up to the hearse.

Sugar tapped on my window. I gulped. Why was Sugar there? Was he part of Marla Maria's harem of men? I rolled down the window.

"Hello darlin'," Sugar's tone dripped with a Southern drawl. He tugged on the edges of his pleather jacket sleeves. "You pickin' up a body? I've always been interested in the afterlife." He dragged his fat finger along the window seal of my car door. There was a big gold ring on it.

"Sugar is hitting on you." Chicken winked like it was a possibility I would even *think* of dating Sugar. Chicken had lost his mind. "He's a good man."

"I don't think my business here is any of your business." I tried not to look at the black lines running down the sides of his face. I pointed up to his face. "You have some sort of black stuff . . ." I raked my fingertips down my temple to show him.

He pulled the handkerchief from his pocket and dabbed the sides of his face.

"Damn stuff." Sugar glanced in my side mirror, coming closer to my window. He didn't need to bend down since his height was perfectly even with the door.

"Is that the spray-on hair?" I couldn't stop myself from asking. "Like the infomercial?" A smile cracked my face. I always wondered who bought the As Seen On TV stuff. Now I knew—Sugar.

"I told him not to buy that crap." Chicken couldn't stop laughing.

"It has a guarantee to work." Sugar's hair was dripping faster than he could clean it up.

"Well Sugar, I guess you shouldn't believe everything you see on TV," I suggested.

He jerked up and glared at me. "How do you know my name?"

Crap.

"Oh, oh." Chicken chose this moment to get serious. "He is really smart. Not a dumb one. Sugar Wayne is the smartest friend I have."

"You told me." I never had a good poker face.

"Darlin', I never said my name." Sugar didn't worry about the dripping black fake hair. The spurs jingled as he leaned against the hearse and crossed his ankles. "I think you need to come clean as to why you are here at my dead friend's house."

"Did you say dead friend?" I asked. "I'm here to talk to the family about pre-need arrangements."

I grabbed a piece of paper out of the glove box and pretended to read Chicken's address off it.

"Oh no." I did a quick show of the paper so he

really couldn't read what I flashed and threw it back in the glove box. "This paper is old. I must've grabbed the wrong sheet from the funeral home." I shrugged. "Silly me."

"I still didn't say my name." Sugar's eyes dipped, his brows followed.

"Thank you!" I waved and put the hearse in reverse before I punched it. Gravel spit from underneath the wheels, making dust fly all over Sugar. His dripping hair was now a dull gray from the mix of the dust and black.

Looking in the rearview mirror, I noticed that Sugar didn't take his eyes off the hearse until we turned out of the trailer park.

Chapter 7

"What was that?" Chicken turned his body in the seat and looked back at the trailer park, which was fast disappearing in the background as I sped toward Sleepy Hollow.

"That was me getting the hell out of Dodge." I gripped the wheel hard as the hearse hugged the curves of the back road. Hearses were not meant to go fast and I had the sucker floored. And there was no need for Chicken to tell me to keep my eyes on the road.

"Go back!" Chicken screamed at me as we barreled back to town. "He was there to check on Lady Cluckington."

My phone beeped from the seat. I glanced over to see it was Granny texting something about her scooter. Instead of trying to decode her message, I decided to pay her a visit. Yoga was on my agenda, and maybe Hettie Bell was there and I could talk some sense into her nonsense of this yoga epidemic she'd started with the Auxiliary women.

"What do you mean he was there to check on Lady?" I asked, wondering if my fear made me a little too hasty in getting away.

"He knows how much Marla Maria hates Lady. Over a beer one night at the Watering Hole, I told him that if anything ever happened to me he had to look after Lady because I knew Marla Maria wasn't going to hold to her end of the agreement."

That was the second time he'd mentioned the Watering Hole. I was definitely going to have to check it out now.

"Tell me about the agreement," I begged. "You've mentioned the agreement a million times, but you haven't told me what was in the agreement."

"It's in writing." Chicken's eyes grew big. "I might not have had a will, but I read somewhere on the library computer Internet that you could write an agreement and sign it. Good as a will."

"What did the agreement say?" I was losing my patience. Granted, Chicken was a good ol' country boy and he really did believe a handwritten agreement was good, but it was no good if only he and Marla Maria knew about it. If she had to hold up to some part of the deal in order to get something, then why would she share the agreement? I was beginning to realize Marla Maria wasn't as stupid as she wanted us to think.

"I have a bit of money." Chicken hesitated and eyeballed me.

"The real estate?" I asked.

Chicken's mouth flew open, and then he snapped it closed. "You ain't going to tell no one that I got some money, are you?"

"Depends." Did he forget he was a ghost and that he asked me to find out who murdered him? "If Marla Maria knows you have money, that could be a motive to kill you."

"Uh." Chicken's mouth dropped. "You think she'd kill me for the money?"

"You had an agreement, didn't you?"

"Huh." Chicken's mouth dropped again. The creases around his eyes deepened into a frown.

"Did the agreement have anything to do with the money?" Not that the end result about money wasn't enough of a motive, but I had to know what Marla Maria had to do to get the money. "Did she have to follow through with something in order to get the money?"

"Marla Maria has to take care of Lady Cluck-ington just like I did in order to get the money."

"What do you mean 'take care of'?" I asked.

At this point in the investigation, I had to get the particulars. Every single detail mattered.

"Marla has to feed her, bathe her, groom her, and keep her cage clean." As he read off Marla's chores again, he held up his fingers, counting them out. "And she has to enter her into all the prize hen pageants."

I held my hand up in the air to stop him. "You already told me about the chores. Till me more about the pageants." I slowed the hearse down once we made it into the square. There were so many people still setting up for the evening's big festival kickoff. Tonight was the annual hoedown and chicken dinner.

"That's the problem, and that is where Sugar comes in." Chicken peered out the window. "Marla never went to the pageants with me so she had never seen how to show a prize hen as fine as Lady."

Chicken paused. He swallowed back tears.

"Are you okay?" I asked pulling into the Sleepy Hollow Inn. I put my phone up to my ear to pretend to talk on it. I didn't want to risk anyone seeing me and telling Granny I had another case of the Funeral Trauma. "I know it's hard to relive all of this, but in order for me to mark Marla Maria off the suspect list, I need to know everything."

Unfortunately, the more he told me, the more Marla Maria looked guilty.

"I'm sure Sugar was there to get Lady for practice. The big state fair is coming up and it's a surefire way to get into the national competition coming up in three months." He smacked his fist on the dashboard. "I'm sure Marla Maria is avoiding Sugar. I never wrote in the agreement that she couldn't avoid Sugar. Marla is a smart one." He tapped his temple. "She ain't no dummy."

"Let me get this straight." Getting Chicken to tell me what the agreement was about was like pulling candy out of a kid's hand. "You have this land in Lexington that is worth money. The agreement states that Marla Maria has to take care of Lady exactly like you did, but Sugar is the one who is to take Lady to the pageants and show her?"

He nodded.

"And Marla Maria knows that if she isn't home, Sugar can't make good on his promise?" I had to get clear, straight answers. Especially before my romantic dinner with Jack Henry. The quicker we get Chicken back in the ground, the faster I can get on with my love life and future with Jack.

"Yes. Sugar is a realtor in Lexington. I bought the property from him years ago. We became fast friends." Chicken had a faraway look in his eyes. "Marla Maria never hid her feelings about Lady. Over the years, Marla Maria got more and more jealous. Every day she said nasty things about me and Lady." He swallowed hard. "Sugar and I were getting Lady ready for a show and Marla Maria told us that she wished Lady would get out of her cage and claw our eyes out with her talons."

"Wow. That's harsh." Need I remind him of a woman scorned? Only this time it was by a chicken.

"That's not all." Worry crept into Chicken's eyes. "After Sugar and I got Lady loaded up and on the road, she got out of her cage and flapped all around, almost causing us to wreck."

I gasped. Marla Maria was looking guiltier by the minute.

"When I got the car under control and pulled over, I went back to investigate how Lady got out of her cage." Chicken shook his head like he was trying to shake the memory from his mind. "Someone had cut the lock."

"Didn't you put Lady in the car and then get in?" Something wasn't adding up. How did he not see someone cut a lock?

"Sugar and I went back in to grab a snack for the road. I had no idea where Marla Maria was because I walked around yelling for her trying to tell her good-bye." He sucked in a deep breath. "I have a secret video camera system installed. No one knows about it."

"What?" My mouth dropped.

"Yeah." He grumbled. "Lady didn't win the show because she was still so upset about being loose in the car. Prize hens don't like to be in cars. I went home and rolled back the video tape. Marla Maria was walking away from the car when Sugar and I were inside getting a snack."

My heart dropped. I truly didn't want to believe that Marla Maria had anything to do with Chicken's death. Memories of them flooded my mind. I recalled how proud he was when Marla was by his side. He even looked like a proud banty rooster with his prize chicken. Not that he looked like a rooster nor she like a chicken, but it seemed fitting.

"There you are!" Granny yelled from the front porch of the Inn. My eyes glanced over to the big tree in the yard. Granny's moped was chained up to the tree with a heavy-duty industrial chain and lock.

"We will talk in a minute," I told Chicken, and

put my phone down before I got out of the hearse. There were so many more questions I needed to ask about the agreement and the property.

"Morning ladies," I stood at the bottom of the Inn steps and said hello to Mable Claire, Granny, Beulah Paige and Hettie Bell. I felt I should keep a safe distance from the four of them doing God-knowswhat to their bodies. Plus, I had heard some of those positions made some people pass gas, and I didn't want to be downwind from any of them. Granny included. "What are y'all doing?"

The women were in the downward dog position. The only yoga position I knew other than the Prasarita Padottanasana pose that Beulah had demonstrated.

"We are getting in touch with our feelings." Mable Claire waddled up to stand. Her fuller hips jingled from coins in her pocket. Mable Claire could be heard before she came into view. As long as I could remember, she loaded her pockets down with change and handed out a dime here and there to children she saw. "You know"—she picked at the bun on the top of her head—"you should join the Auxiliary. We'd love to have you."

Beulah popped up. If the downward dog was supposed to calm her, it wasn't working. Mable

Claire's suggestion of me joining the Auxiliary made Beulah as nervous as a cat in a roomful of rocking chairs.

"You can't ask someone to join the Auxiliary, Mable Claire." Beulah scolded poor old Mable. "She has to be formally checked out and an invitation sent. We have to vote on who we invite."

"We know Emma Lee. She's a pillar of the community, not to mention"—Mable Claire gave me a theatrical wink—"she has that hot hunky Jack Henry by her side. I personally wouldn't mind having him as a speaker at our meeting on how to stay safe in our unsafe town."

"Unsafe town?" I asked.

"Oh yes." Mable Claire's eyes darted around to each of us. "Zula told us about the murder charges against Marla Maria."

"Granny!" My jaw dropped. She had gone and done it now. Jack Henry was going to be spitting mad when . . . when . . . It was probably already around town about Chicken Teater. Not that everyone wasn't going to find out soon anyway. It wasn't like the warrant wasn't public record. It was just a matter of time.

"What? I told Mable Claire. I can't help it if other people were eavesdropping on our conversation."

"Are you talking about me?" Beulah looked up from her contorted position that I was sure was not a yoga pose.

"If the shoe fits," Granny chimed as she changed position trying to mimic Hettie Bell.

"Now ladies," Hettie warned, planting her forehead on the ground with her arms stretched out in front of her. "Concentrate on this pose. It will calm you."

"I'm not sure I can sit on my thighs like that." Mable Claire referred to the childlike pose Hettie was trying to get them to do.

I watched as they followed Hettie's lead. It was as if they had been brainwashed.

"Stinkin' thinkin' is not welcome here ladies." Hettie took a deep breath through her nose and released a rush of air out of her mouth.

"*Ridiculous,*" I murmured under my breath. "Have you lost your mind?" I climbed the steps to the porch. They had moved all of the welcoming rockers and beautiful planters for the guests to enjoy. "Jack Henry doesn't know if Chicken was murdered or not. There was some paperwork that didn't add up." I did my best to cover up Granny's loose lips. The older she got, the worse she got. I didn't want her taking over as president and CEO of the Sleepy Hollow gossip mill. "It was four years ago."

"Still." Beulah put her hands on her hips, making her bangles clink together. Her silk jump-suit glistened in the afternoon sun. "An unsolved murder means there is a murderer out there."

"This is not good." I shook my head.

"Emma Lee, everyone in town knew that some-thing was wrong when the police put up yellow tape." Granny craned her neck in a position that I didn't ever want to try. "But when they dug up a grave"—Granny reared back her head—"that was another story."

"We will see what kind of modern-day foren-sics you get from that fancy company you pleaded with the city to spend their extra dollars on." Beulah gave her shit-eatin' grin.

Beulah was the first one at the council meet-ing to protest when I suggested we use the extra taxpayers' dollars to spend on the latest foren-sics equipment for the police station. Granted, Eternal Slumber's morgue had always been the site the Sleepy Hollow Police Department used way before I had taken over and way before Jack Henry was my boyfriend. It was a deal my dad had made in his younger days.

The equipment we had was outdated. Sleepy Hollow had spent even more money sending off any type of forensic things they needed and I actually saved the city money. Regardless, the equipment was approved and Vernon Baxter was happy about it. Especially now, since we needed to do some of that fancy extracting from Chicken Teater's four-year-old decayed bones.

"Focus, ladies." Hettie Bell ignored me and did some sort of long breathing which I was sure was because her pants and top were too tight. Looking at her made me have shallow breath.

Granny, Beulah and Mable all took a deep breath at the same time. *Hot air*. I glared at them.

"Yep, y'all have lost your minds." I pointed to each of them. "You too, Hettie Bell."

"Ohmm . . ." Hettie spewed some jibber jabber from her gut.

"Oh stop it, Hettie." I rolled my eyes.

Granny took a deep breath and stood up, following Hettie to a tee. "We are doing this so we don't lose our minds." Granny swooped back down lifting her head high in the air.

"It's not working." I pointed to the tree. "You have completely lost it and the chained-up scooter proves it."

"That is why I called you." Granny did a little

hop. Her feet were planted under her. Her arms did a fluid motion up to each side. She clasped her hands over her head. "I need you to find the spare key to my motorcycle in the funeral-home office. I've misplaced my keys or someone has stolen them." Her eyes focused on me. "One of them little campers." She pointed up to the mountainous caves that were the backdrop for the Inn.

It was the most beautiful picture. That was why the Inn was so valuable. It was a perfect spot for visitors to rest their tired heads after a day of hiking the caves and gorge. Plus the dining room was seated on the back side of the Inn. The entire back wall was glass and had a picturesque view like no other in Sleepy Hollow.

"Keys? As in all your keys?" I asked.

"Ummhmm." Granny didn't bother opening her eyes.

"As in the keys to the Inn, Eternal Slumber, hearse . . ." Holy crap! They had to be somewhere. Had. To. Be.

"Ummhmm," she repeated, like it was not a big deal that every single key was on there.

"Where did you have them last?" I snapped at Granny. My temper was beginning to flare.

"Where I always put them." Granny cocked up one eyebrow when she took in a deep breath through her nose. She released the air. She positioned herself to talk to the other women and made the motion as if she had keys in her hand. "Hanging on the hook in the kitchen. Not there now. I needed to go to Artie's for some more eggs for that delicious egg-and-ham-omelet casserole, you know Mary Anna Hardy's recipe that she brings to people's layout dinners." All the women nodded. The Auxiliary women loved to bring their best dishes to feed mourners at funerals. The better your dish, the higher in society you were. Granny was known for her good country cooking and Mary Anna wasn't going to pass her up. No doubt in my mind that Granny wasn't putting her own spin on the recipe to make it better for the next funeral.

Their eyes grew as big as their stomachs when Granny mentioned food.

Granny continued, "Anyway, I had to walk all the way there and back," she said as if it were a far place, not something through the square, which was across the street. A five-minute walk at the most. She rubbed the small of her back. "I know someone had their eye on my motorcycle, so while I was there I had Artie deliver me a chain and lock. No one is going to steal my cycle." Her lashes lowered, creating a shadow over her cheeks.

"It's not a motorcycle! It's a moped! Geez, move it." I barreled my way through their yoga mats to the front door of the Inn, knocking Beulah square on her silk covered butt. Under my breath I said, "I can't believe you are worried about that old dime-store moped."

Granny thought she hit gold when she came back from the Lexington flea market riding the moped. She boasted how it was only fifty dollars after she traded in her car, and she could get around town for pennies of gas. Little did she realize she wasn't good at staying upright on two wheels. Every week, I got endless complaints about Granny almost running people over.

"Out of my way! Old lady riding a motorcycle!" She would yell right before she was about to hit someone. Jack Henry even came to see me about it, but there was nothing I could do about Zula Fae Raines Payne. Granny was set in her ways and not even hunky Jack was going to sweet-talk her into going back to driving a car.

"Zula Fae Raines Payne, didn't you teach your granddaughter better manners than that?" Beulah huffed and puffed.

I didn't wait around to see if Granny had defended me. I had to find her keys. The last thing I needed was to worry about someone stealing the hearse . . . or worse . . . breaking into Eternal Slumber now that everyone knew there was a murder. Eternal Slumber was on high alert, especially now with the new forensic equipment. Four years was a long time in the detective department.

I bet the killer didn't figure little ol' Sleepy Hollow would invest in some high-tech equipment where we could figure out decade-old murders. Or had I been watching too many TV detective shows? Either way, anything could happen, and I needed to find those keys.

The white front double doors were wide open and Granny had the screen doors put in to let in the constant flow of fresh air. Since Sleepy Hollow was just that—a deep hollow—we had a beautiful and refreshing breeze all year round.

Recently, Granny had redecorated by painting the entire inside a more subtle and homey tan color. She replaced all the old Victorian furniture with a more modern look of printed fabrics and leather. She did a fabulous job and everyone in town loved it. The Inn guests always told Granny how comfortable staying there was.

I walked back down the hallway and glanced up at the stairs as I passed. There were some guests coming down with large backpacks filled to the gills. They disappeared into the room on the right, which Granny used as a common area for the guests, and she kept snacks there all day long.

I swung the kitchen door open. There was a hook nailed to the wall where Granny kept her keys so she wouldn't lose them. *Some luck she's had with that*. The hook was empty, just like Granny said. I walked around the kitchen counter looking for the set of keys.

The old farm table in the middle of the room was filled with flour bags and all sorts of ingredients, along with a written recipe from *The Kitchen of Mary Anna Hardy;* at least that was what the recipe card had printed on it. Good Southern women always kept their recipes on personalized stationery and in a fabric box. Me? I relied on good old McDonald's to feed me—but not tonight.

My mouth watered for a taste of delicious bread from Bella Vino and Jack Henry's lips on mine. The thought made me tingle.

"Is that Zula's sweet tea?" Chicken Teater stood by the window where Granny had set a pitcher of her famous sweet tea in the early morning sun. She claimed the sun helped bring out the natural flavor of the tea, but we all knew it was the pound of sugar that made her sweet tea to die for.

"It sure is." The golden orange color was so inviting, any time of the day. "We don't have time to have a cup of tea."

"If I could drink it, that entire pitcher would be gone." Chicken rubbed his hands on the pitcher.

Buzz. The timer on the oven brought me back to the reality of why we were in the Inn's kitchen. Granny's keys. *Buzz.*

I grabbed a potholder and pulled down the oven door. Granny's version of Mary Anna Hardy's omelet casserole looked "to die for" with the crispy brown top and bubbling sides. I reached in, pulled it out and set the dish on the baking rack Granny used for cooling her dishes.

"I really miss doing this with Lady."

I jumped around. I still wasn't used to hearing voices of people who weren't in the physical world. Chicken Teater was blowing a feather through the kitchen.

I grabbed it out of the air.

"Where did you get that?" It was a real feather, right here in Granny's kitchen. Granny would never have a feather in her kitchen. I surveyed the gold and black feather, bringing it closer to my face.

"It was over there next to the door. Lady Cluckington and I used to run around the chicken coop blowing feathers." He chuckled. "Well, I blew the feathers and she would try to grab them with that sweet little beak."

"Okaaay . . ." I drew the word out as I put my hand in the air and shook my head. There was no time for strolling down memory lane. "This could be a clue. Show me exactly where you found it."

"You sure are a testy Raines." Reluctantly, he walked back toward the door and pointed directly underneath the hook where the keys always hung. "You sure don't have your parents' personality."

"Leave my parents out of this. They are enjoying their retired life in Florida." I walked over and bent down to the place where he said he found the feather. The small dirt footprint wasn't visible unless you squatted down. "Marla Maria," I whispered and took my phone out of my back pocket.

I took a quick picture for evidence. Granny would have a fit if she knew there was a dirty shoe in her kitchen.

"You think?" Chicken stood over the print.

"Move," I ordered and snapped a couple more pictures at different angles. "You are blocking my view. Do I think what?"

"You think that little bit of dirt is Marla Maria's?"

I looked up. Chicken had tears in his eyes. I stood up and rubbed his arm—well, as best as one can rub a ghost's arm—for some sort of comfort.

"It has to be hard to think that the one and only woman you married and poured your heart into, the love of your life, would ever harm you." I knew it wasn't much comfort, but it was all I had in me. I put my phone and the feather in my pocket. Neither Granny nor the Auxiliary women needed to know what I had found out.

My nerves gurgled at the thought of going back to Marla Maria's, but I knew I had to. I had to break in when she wasn't home and search for those clues.

"Marla Maria?" Chicken slapped his knee and broke out in a fit of laughter. "Love of my life?" He pointed at me before he bent over cackling some more. "Lady Cluckington is the love of my life."

"You were just crying," I pointed out.

"Because, the thought that that woman would hurt my Lady hurts my heart. Hell, Marla Maria had filed divorce papers on me a week before I died. If I'd known I was going to die, I would've torn up the agreement." Chicken disappeared into thin air.

"Where are you?" I twirled around. "You can't just drop bombs on me and leave." I gestured between myself and the air and loudly whispered, "This is not how this gig works."

"Who are you talking to?" Granny stood at the swinging door with her hands on her hips.

"You." I bit my lip.

Her eyes narrowed. "I wasn't in here." She lifted the back of her hand and put it on my forehead to check and see if I had a fever. I jerked away. "You got the Funeral Trauma again?" She stomped out of the kitchen. I followed her. She spouted, "I knew digging up Chicken Teater wasn't going to be good on your health. I'm calling Doc Clyde."

"Granny I'm fine. I was talking about your keys. You can't just drop a bomb on me about your keys and not care." I tried to worm my way out of the sticky situation I had just put myself into.

"I swear. I'm going to give hottie Jack Henry a piece of my mind—after I let him hug me—when I see him." Granny fanned herself with her hands and we walked out the front door of the Inn.

"Now, now." Beulah straightened up. "Doc Clyde said not to get your blood pressure up."

"Blood pressure?" Was Granny confiding in Beulah Paige now? That was odd.

Granny gave Beulah the stink eye. Beulah looked away and dove down into a downward dog. I wasn't going to argue with her. I just wanted to get out of this frying pan and jump into another one. Marla Maria's.

I trotted down the steps.

"I'm going to find those keys." I turned around once I got to the bottom. "Oh, I'd love to attend the next Auxiliary meeting." I grinned, knowing Beulah's heart had just stopped. "And Granny," I tapped my temple, "I almost forgot. Your timer dinged about . . ." I glanced at my empty wrist like I had a watch on. " . . . ten minutes ago."

"If my casserole is burnt . . ." Granny rushed back into the Inn muttering something under her breath.

"Namaste!" I yelled before I got back into the hearse.

Chapter 8

By the time I got back to Eternal Slumber and logged all clues I had gathered from my little adventures, it was time to get ready for my date with Jack Henry.

"Where are you going?" Charlotte Rae stood behind me as I locked my office door. "It's only four."

I jiggled the handle. If there was someone on the loose with the keys, I had to tell Charlotte. Something I wasn't looking forward to doing.

"I . . . I . . ." I fought hard to find the words that weren't going to send her over the edge. "I think you need to sit down. In your office." I pointed up the hall toward her door.

"Tell me what you have done now." Her green

eyes pierced through me just like Granny's did when she thought I was up to no good.

"Me?" I was tired of taking the fall for Granny and her tomfoolery.

"Oh God." Charlotte put her hands to her heart. "I guess I better sit down if it's about Granny."

Instead of going into Charlotte's office, we headed to the vestibule. The chairs were set up for the funeral of an elderly local who had been sick for a long time. Still, the whole town would be here to pay their respects. That was probably why Granny was working on a casserole.

The old wooden folding chairs looked lovely all lined up. I had yet to put the cream cotton slipcovers on them. They were still at the cleaners being pressed in all the right places. Although it was a funeral, we made sure it was just as nice as a wedding. After all, funerals and weddings in Sleepy Hollow were celebrated in the same fashion. Big.

The chairs creaked when we sat down.

"Granny has lost her keys." I had to say it like you rip off a Band-Aid. Fast.

"She what?" Charlotte jumped up, flipping the chair backward. "You mean *all* her keys?"

I slowly nodded. Trust me. The old saying "never make a redhead mad" was true. Charlotte Rae was on fire from head to toe. She thrust her hands to her side and tugged on the edges of her suit coat before she whipped around and headed to the elevator. She stood with her back to me. I swear she was shaking. When the elevator picked her up, she stomped inside and never turned back around.

Charlotte knew without saying, she had to go tell Vernon about the breach of security. There was no doubt Granny had put us in a bad spot. Thankfully, it was her job to make sure she got the locks changed and I could go get ready for my date.

Dom, dom, dom. Chopin's "Funeral March" chimed on my cell. I smiled when I saw it was Jack Henry. No matter how bad my day had gone, seeing his name made everything all better.

"I can taste Bella Vino's red wine right now," I answered the phone with excitement.

"About that." Jack Henry didn't sound as upbeat as me. In fact, I could tell what was coming next. "I'm going to have to cancel."

"Why?" My heart sank. I sat back in the chair further.

"It seems like the media found out we are investigating a murder involving Chicken and they are now camped out at the trailer park. Marla Maria called me for some help."

"Oh, that's all right." I was lying through my teeth. It was far from all right.

"Are you sure you're okay?" He didn't even pause for me to answer. "She said she was swarmed."

I had totally forgotten about the media. I got up and pulled the curtains back. A little bit of dust puffed off the drapes. I made a mental note to dust them before the funeral tomorrow. Jack Henry was right. There wasn't a camera around.

"Well I'll be," I said. "I got back here a little bit ago and didn't even notice they were gone."

In reality, I bet Marla Maria was loving the attention. What beauty queen didn't?

"Do you know how the media found out?" Jack Henry asked. I couldn't tell if he was baiting me or really asking me.

"Granny?" I closed my eyes, my jaw tensed.

"You got it." There was a pause in his voice. "Did you happen to tell Zula about the investigation?"

"No. No I didn't." I didn't really lie to Jack Henry because I didn't tell Granny. "Seriously? Do you think people don't know what is going on when you dig up a four-year-old corpse?"

"I guess you're right. But I didn't want to deal with this and the festival all at once." Jack Henry sounded exhausted. "Listen, maybe we can meet up at the hoedown tonight."

The hoedown. I had completely forgotten about it. So I did have something to do tonight.

"Sounds good." I let him off the hook. He was under enough stress as it was and I didn't need to add to it. "I do have some interesting news to tell you."

"Is it about the investigation?" Jack Henry didn't want to be bothered with my everyday trauma of Granny.

"Granny's lost her keys or they got stolen." I was about to tell him about the feather in the kitchen and the agreement, but he interrupted me.

"Call the station and have Zula file a report." In the background, I could hear his siren go off. "I'm here and need to go."

The line went dead and so did the beat of my heart.

Chapter 9

There wasn't much more spying I was going to be able to do on Marla Maria since the media was there and she had my Jack over there to protect her, which made me somewhat jealous. Figuring out how to get the agreement was on my mind, but since my stomach was growling so loud it could wake the dead, I decided to venture over to the square. The Cattlemen's Association burgers didn't sound so bad after all.

I made sure the doors to Eternal Slumber were locked up tight before I walked across the street. The quartet was in harmony heaven with the sweet sounds echoing all through the hollow, and most of the town was gathered around the gazebo, eating and drinking.

"Zula for mayor!" The group of Auxiliary women marched in a circle raising signs in the air with Granny leading the pack. "Zula for mayor!"

I dodged them and headed straight for the burger stand. The last thing I wanted to do was hold a sign up all night and that was what would happen if Granny saw me. She would expect me to do the right thing and get the word out.

I could hear her now—*Emma Lee, we are family. Family sticks by one another*—while she stuck a sign in my face.

"There's no stopping her." Hettie Bell walked up and nudged me when I was in line. She had on her capri pants and light blue button-down, topped off with her white high-top Converse tennis shoes.

"You aren't helping matters." I shook my head and looked down at my boring jeans, black T-shirt and Sperry Top-Siders.

"Me?" Hettie pulled back. "What did I do?"

"All that positive energy you claim she's getting and all the peaceful-breathing crap don't help." I pretended to do some sort of yoga pose, which I was not good at. "I like Granny's Southern ways without the calming crap added in. She looks crazy running around town doing the downward dog in every line she's in."

"She was doing some crazy stretch when she was in line at Artie's Deli and Meats earlier when I was there picking up supplies for our camping trip," the person in front of us turned around and said. "Nice town by the way. Looking forward to exploring the caves."

"See?" I pointed to the stranger. "They don't even live here and noticed her."

"She's fine." Hettie tried to assure me. She knew just as much as I did, that when Granny did something she went full force. Yoga included. "Maybe I can tone it down a bit."

"A bit?" I questioned. "A lot, please." I rolled my eyes.

I didn't mind Granny getting into shape with yoga, but all the mumbo jumbo *namaste* junk was going a little overboard.

"Truce?" Hettie put her hand out.

"Truce." I took it and shook. "But I want you to come to the Watering Hole with me tonight."

"Eww." Her button nose curled. She tucked a strand of hair behind her ear. She fidgeted. "That place is nasty. Why on earth would you want to go there?"

"I need to go see what it's all about." I took a step forward. I was next in line. "Let's just say it's for research."

"Research?" Hettie's eyes narrowed. A smile crossed her face. "Does this have anything to do with why they dug up that man?"

"I said research." There was no way I was going to tell Hettie what was going on. Like I said, I barely knew her since she was new in town, but there were possibilities of a friendship. Well, depending on if she went to the Watering Hole with me, which would be a total "friend" thing. "Are you going to go with me?"

"You buying?" she asked.

"Sure." I agreed, but didn't even think about how much that was going to cost me. If I had anything to do with it, I was hoping Sugar was going to be there. At least that was where Chicken had said Sugar liked to hang out, and with a little liquor in him, I was sure it would give him some loose lips. It would be very interesting to hear his version of the marriage of Chicken, Marla Maria and Lady Cluckington.

After I ordered my burger, I told Hettie Bell I would grab a picnic table near the little Higher Grounds Café booth. It was still in eyeshot of Granny, but far enough away so Granny wouldn't be able to distinguish me from all the other people.

"She sure is serious about becoming mayor." Cheryl Lynn had a blinking button on her shirt.

The on and off lights spelled ZULA in red dots. She put a cup of coffee in front of me. "You are going to need a lot of this to keep up."

"Yes you are." Mary Anna Hardy came up from behind us. She had on her best Marilyn Monroe look—the flirty little white dress, high heels, boobs propped up to her chin and bright red lips all completed by her bleached-blond hair teased to heaven. Higher the hair, higher to God, was Mary Anna's motto. She set her plate of barbecue on the table and quickly raked her hands through her blond hair, making it even bigger. "Zula is not going to let O'Dell Burns take the position."

"You could probably take him out for her using your shoes," I teased and took a big ol' bite out of my burger, which was not to be compared to Bella Vino's. If I squeezed my eyes really tight, I felt like I was there.

"She sure could use them. She'd get the job done." Mary Anna winked. "You know my Marilyn always says"—she did the sign of the cross before she paid tribute to her icon—"Give a girl the right pair of shoes and she will conquer the world. No doubt in my mind that Zula could rule the world and more if she put on these shoes."

"Don't give her the chance," I warned Mary Anna. "Say, I need to come in and get a trim."

"You sure do." Her eyes moved around my head. She plunged her fingers deep in my brown hair. "You are getting a tad bit mousey."

I jerked away. Jack Henry's fingers were the only fingers I wanted in my hair.

"Thanks," I grumbled underneath my breath and took another bite of my burger. I really didn't want to get my hair done, but I needed to get in the chair to hear all the ramblings of Chicken and Marla Maria.

"I've got an opening tomorrow." She couldn't resist sticking her fingers back in my hair. "You need a brow wax too."

"You ready?" I eyed Hettie Bell when she walked up.

"After I finish my burger." Her eyes narrowed.

Before she could sit down between Mary Anna and Cheryl Lynne, I jumped up and grabbed her by the elbow.

"Take it with you." I smiled at the girls. "See y'all tomorrow."

"What was that about?" Hettie jerked away once we were out of sight and across the street on the sidewalk in front of Eternal Slumber.

"Mary Anna was all in my hair and made me an appointment with her tomorrow." I walked up the steps with Hettie following. I unlocked the door and pushed it open.

"You could use a little touch-up." Hettie Bell's eyes focused on my outgrown highlights.

"Shut up." I stepped inside the vestibule. I had to get my keys to the hearse. "Come on." I held the door open for her and flicked on the lights.

"Nope." She shook her head.

"Nope what?"

"I'm not going in there." She pointed to the inside of the funeral home. "Dead people are in there."

"What do you think they are going to do? Talk to you?" I kind of laughed but secretly wished she was a Betweener and knew my pain.

"I'll stand right here and eat my burger." She held it up in front of her.

"Fine. I'll grab my keys and be right back." I shut the door behind me. I had no idea why people were always so scared of a funeral home. Granted, I had been around it all my life, and before I was a Betweener, I still didn't understand it.

The dead were the last thing anyone had to be afraid of. Now that I was a Betweener, I saw first-hand that ghosts didn't haunt you. They wanted to get on with their afterlife just as much as the living wanted to get on with their lives.

"Charlotte?" I called out when I heard the back door close. The back door was the employee entrance, which was next to my little apartment. Granted, it was more of an efficiency, complete with a bedroom, kitchenette, bathroom and small television room. It was plenty enough for me. Just the perfect size for cuddling with Jack Henry.

I walked to the back to see why Charlotte was here. After I told her about Granny losing her keys, Charlotte decided to go home early to beat the crowd that was expected for the opening ceremony in the square, but I knew her all too well. I was sure the news of the lost keys sent Charlotte Rae straight to bed.

"Charlotte?" The back door was standing wide open. I grabbed my cell from my pocket and called Jack Henry. "I think someone has broken into the funeral home."

"What?" Jack sounded confused. I could hear Marla Maria cackling in the background. "Who?"

"Is that your little funeral girl?" I heard Marla giggle a little too close to the phone.

"Jack Henry, why are you in Marla's double-wide?" There was a sense of urgency in my voice as a jealous tick crept in my soul. "Don't you piss on my leg and tell me it's raining, Jack Henry Ross. You tell me why you aren't outside taking care of the *press*."

Tears started to sting my eyes. Marla Maria might be older than us, but she sure was pretty. Not to mention a beauty queen. And a cougar.

"Is that little boy trying to hit on my Marla Maria?" Chicken Teater stood next to me in the back hallway winding up his arm again.

"No." I shook my head. "I don't think so."

"You don't think what?" Jack Henry asked in the phone.

"Nothing!" I pushed the END button. I didn't care if he came to my rescue. I was mad. Marla Maria was trying to dig her talons into my man. I turned to Chicken. "And you!" I pointed. "Where have you been? Were you here? Did you see who was in here? Did they touch your body?"

"Stop throwing your hissy fit. This isn't going to find out who killed me." Chicken tried to calm me but my heart was racing a mile a minute.

"If it weren't for you, Jack Henry wouldn't be over there protecting your harlot!" I shouted and darted back down the hall to see if anything had been taken. "I have got to figure out what happened to you so Marla Maria can go rot in jail!"

There was no time to spare. Getting to the Watering Hole and gathering evidence was the next step and Hettie was still waiting out front.

Whoever was here couldn't get to the basement where Chicken's body was, because there were only three people who had an elevator key; Charlotte, Vernon, and me. We took that one away from Granny when we caught her doing makeup on a client, Bessie Sue Knoll, when she knew good and well Mary Anna was the cosmetologist of the funeral home. Granny didn't care.

Poor old Bessie Sue Knoll had laid there looking like she had fallen face forward in a clown's makeup bag.

"Keys." I gasped and rushed into Charlotte's office. Her desk drawers had been pulled out and dumped all over the floor. "Granny's extra keys," I groaned.

There was nothing I could do about it until tomorrow, because anyone who could change out the locks would be over at the square tonight. Plus the stores were closed and I wouldn't be able to get new locks anyway.

My office was still locked. I unlocked it and grabbed the hearse keys.

"Hettie." I rushed to the porch. "Did you see anyone run away from the back?"

"No," Hettie said. She was standing on the sidewalk talking to Mable Claire. There were so many people walking around, whoever broke in could blend in easily.

"Marla Maria didn't kill me." Chicken stood next to me looking intently.

"Hold on." I held up a finger and walked back inside. Chicken followed. "What do you mean she didn't kill you? She's my number-one suspect."

"Wasn't she just all over your little no good sheriff?" He put an image in my head that made my blood boil. "How could she be in two places at once?"

"You're right." My eyes popped open. I bit the corner of my lip. Marla Maria couldn't have been the one to break into Eternal Slumber since Jack Henry was *protecting* her, but that didn't mean she didn't kill Chicken. Marla Maria had her hand in Chicken's death. I paced back and forth trying to recall all the clues. "Agreement, divorce, money— half a million in real estate is the prize." I shook my head. "None of this adds up." I snapped my fingers. "John Deere guy!"

"Who?" Chicken followed close on my heels as I walked up and down the hall.

I stopped. Chicken nearly walked right through me.

"The guy with the John Deere hat." I went back to my office, unlocked the door and flipped on the light. I went straight over to my little notebook and opened it. "Here. There was a guy hiding behind a tree while they were digging you up. Remember you told me to look away? Marla Maria *baby*."

Chicken nodded, doing the one-two punch in the air. "That little twit. I showed him."

"Is he in cahoots with Marla Maria?" I started to jot down what I was thinking. "The whole media put a damper on her plan and she told that guy to come here and check out what we had figured out using the new forensic equipment."

"I told you that boy was more slippery than snot on a doorknob." Chicken smacked his hands together. "I bet he was the one who turned my Marla Maria against me and put all them ideas in her head."

"Don't you worry, Chicken." I looked up at him after I scratched a few more notes on my notepad. "I'm going to bring whoever murdered you to justice."

"There ain't nothin' that can't be fixed with a glass of sweet tea." Chicken licked his lips. "I sure wish I had me a big ol' glass."

There was a burning fire in my gut. Not only was I going to put Marla Maria in jail for murder, I was also going to get her claws out of my man.

Chapter 10

Hettie Bell talked and talked *and* talked about the yoga studio all the way to the edge of town where the Watering Hole met the county line. Sleepy Hollow was a dry county, which meant there was no alcohol sold or served at any of the establishments in town. But the next county wasn't and that was where the Watering Hole was strategically placed.

Jack Henry told me that when he joined the sheriff's department, they assigned him to what they called Watering Hole duty. He would sit in his cruiser every single Friday and Saturday night to catch many of the locals who would immediately head to the Watering Hole for a little weekend fun only to drink a little too much fun stuff. When they left, Jack Henry was there to pull them over, give them the Breathalyzer, and haul their drunk butts off to jail.

He said that most of the time, he would put the drunks in the cell for them to sober up and release them the next day.

"Do you think that is a good idea?" Hettie cocked her head to the side and stared at me intently. "Emma Lee, I don't think you were listening to a word I said."

"I was." I could see the old neon cowboy boot half lit up in the distance. It was an icon. In grade school everyone talked about the boot and for as long as I could remember, the lights on it were never all lit at once.

"Then what did I say?" Hettie jerked her head.

"You were telling me about your studio plans." I lied but made it general enough for her to believe me. Clearly, my head wasn't into yoga, nor was my body.

Hettie crossed her arms and gave out a sigh. Evidently, my answer was enough to satisfy her.

I pulled into the gravel lot. There weren't too many cars. I scanned them looking for Sugar Wayne's but it wasn't there. A few motorcycles lined the front. I had heard there were a lot of riders who came here.

"Vroom, vroom." Hettie giggled. "I might find me a Harley man and ride off into the sunset."

"Let me know so I won't be waiting around," I joked, and turned the hearse off. If Sugar Wayne wasn't there, I was wasting my time. My phone buzzed. "Jack." I stuck it back in my pocket.

"You aren't going to answer?" Hettie's eyes grew big. There was never a time I didn't answer a phone call from Jack Henry.

"We are here to have fun!" I yelled and jumped out of the car. My idea of fun was talking to Sugar, hopefully a drunk Sugar, and help get more information on Marla Maria to pin her for Chicken's murder. Then the media would leave and she wouldn't need to be protected by Jack Henry Ross. "Fun," I muttered under my breath before I clicked the key fob to lock the hearse up.

"There a dead body in there?" A lady had jumped off the back of a motorcycle. She had a cigarette tucked in the corner of her mouth that wiggled up and down as she talked. Her eyes squinted from the smoke swirling up around her face. My eyes couldn't get past the Harley shirt shredded on the ends, like she got stuck in a paper shredder, which exposed a large fat roll with stretch marks all over it.

"No." I shook my head and walked past her.

"I'll be dammed!" the woman shouted, catching my attention. "Honey," the woman pointed to me and then to the motorcycle that was pulling into the Watering Hole. The bike looked like a Christmas tree traveling on wheels, there were so many colored lights all over it. "I might kill him tonight so stick around. You might have you a new client." She cackled, leading into such a deep cough I was sure she would fall over dead from not being able to catch her breath.

I almost asked her if she wanted to smoke another cigarette, but I figured being a smart-ass in such an establishment wouldn't make me very popular, since smoke was rolling out of the door when Hettie and I walked in.

"Look how cute this is, Emma Lee!" Hettie Bell ran up to the bar and patted the bar stools, which were disguised as horse saddles.

I smiled and nodded. I was eerily aware that all eyes were on us, not to mention, our attire did not fit in at the Watering Hole. There were five or so men playing billiards on the far end of the small bar. There were only four tables with four chairs and the rest of the seating was along the bar.

"I'll have a cosmopolitan." Hettie plopped her purse on the bar top.

"Y'ull have a what?" The bartender cocked his lip to the right, his mustache twitched a little. He firmly planted his hands on the bar top and leaned his body weight on them, leaning a little closer to Hettie.

"Umm . . ." Hettie nervously stalled, "whatever you have on tap is fine."

"That's what I thought." The man growled, grabbed a glass from the stack and flipped the beer tap, filling the glass to the rim. Hettie and I didn't say a word. He slammed the glass down in front of her. He looked at me. "What do you want?"

"The same is good for me." I gestured to Hettie's drink and moved slightly away from the leather-clad man who popped a squat on the horse saddle next to me. I had to breathe out of my mouth to avoid the smell of cologne the man must have bathed in before he decided to come to such a fine establishment. There was nothing like the smell of cologne and smoke mingled together with beer.

Without acknowledging me, the bartender poured the drink and slid it my way.

"He scares me." Hettie tilted her head to watch the bartender go down to the end of the bar and take care of the Harley momma. The bartender poured her a whiskey shot and one for himself. They cheered and threw the shot back, coming up for a big laugh at the end.

"So does she," I said about the Harley momma.

"You new around here, baby?" The man clinked his glass up against mine.

I pulled my glass closer to me and tried not to look at the man.

"You are that funeral girl." He smacked the counter. I instantly knew who it was when I saw the gold ring. *Sugar.*

"I am a funeral director." I corrected him. Being called funeral girl got old real fast. "Do I know you?" I played dumb.

"Who is your little friend, Emma?" Amusement grew in Hettie's eyes. She threw a cocktail napkin across me and over to Sugar. "You have some black stuff dripping down the side of your face."

"Damn. Damn. Damn." Sugar grabbed the napkin and tried to get off the saddle, only his five-foot frame was too short and he had to jump. He tumbled off, luckily landing on his feet. He rushed off.

"What the hell was that?" Hettie laughed.

"That is why we are here." I picked up my beer and took a gulp. I was going to have to flirt with Sugar Wayne. I smiled when I looked over at Hettie. "Hettie, I need a big favor. I mean big."

"What?" She sounded a little cautious.

I looked to see if Sugar was on his way back, because I had limited time to tell Hettie what she needed to do.

"I need you to flirt with this guy. Get him to drink a lot." I unbuttoned a couple of her buttons. She jerked away.

"Have you lost your mind?" she yelped.

"No." I rushed; Sugar was walking back. "Here, trade me." I got up from my saddle and pushed her over to mine. "Please. It's about the exhumation of that body."

"Shit, Emma Lee." Hettie scooted her beer in front of her. "You okay, darlin'?" she asked Sugar.

He lit up like a firecracker.

"I'm good now." He winked and leaned closer to Hettie before he took a deep inhale. "You sure do smell good. Is that . . ."

"Eau de toilette Bell." Hettie swung her head, making her bob swing from side to side. I grinned, knowing she was referring to her own smell.

"That's it." Sugar grinned. "That's that expensive stuff."

"Ummhmm." Hettie rolled her eyes and took a drink. "So what do you do?"

"Besides drive my big hog?" Sugar winked again. He gave me the creeps; I knew he had to be freaking out Hettie. "I'm Sugar Wayne, the big realtor in Lexington. Sweeten the deal with a little Sugar on it. Haven't you seen my commercials?"

"You are him?" Hettie's mouth dropped. Slowly she turned her head and glared at me. "I didn't know we were in the company of a celebrity. Did you, Emma Lee?"

"Yeah, funeral girl, you need to give me the respect I deserve." Sugar leaned back in the saddle and looked at me behind Hettie's back. "Your lovely friend, and I mean *all* of her is lovely"—his eyes went straight to the unbuttoned part of Hettie's button down—"seems to know a man when she sees one."

"Where?" Hettie yelped.

"Where's what, baby?" Sugar leaned back up against the counter.

"A man," she muttered under her breath toward me. She threw her hand in the air. "I need another drink on him." She pointed to Sugar. Reluctantly, Sugar nodded.

"Don't worry about Emma Lee." Hettie elbowed Sugar. "She keeps to herself."

"As long as she keeps away from me and my love for you." Sugar laid it on thick. I started to feel a little bad for asking Hettie to flirt with him, but I had to have answers about his part of the agreement he had with Chicken. "It's been a bad day, baby."

"He's up to his old tricks." Chicken Teater appeared, standing between Hettie and Sugar with a big grin on his face. "The night I met Marla Maria he was hitting on her. Little did I realize she wanted a date with me. Ask him about the time I met Marla Maria."

"So tell me." I leaned on the bar using my elbows. "What were you doing at Chicken's place earlier?"

"How do you know Chicken?" Sugar questioned and downed the rest of the glass of beer. He smacked the counter. The bartender didn't skip a beat. He had a new glass of brew in front of Sugar in no time.

"He was a friend of my daddy's. Plus my Granny put him in the grave four years ago," I said casually. "And I had to dig him back up today."

Sugar shook his head. "You ought to be ashamed

of yourself for digging up a good man from his resting place after all of these years."

"You knew him well?" Hettie patted Sugar's hand, which was resting on the bar, with a look of disgust on her face.

Sugar took the gesture as if Hettie wanted to hold his hand. He grabbed hers and held it to his heart.

"Knew him?" His eyes glazed over. I couldn't tell if he was getting emotional because Hettie had given him some sort of hope or if he was upset thinking about Chicken. "I was his best friend. Why'd you go digging him up anyways?"

Hettie tried to tug her hand away when Sugar put it on his leg and put his on top, but he held tight.

"I do what I'm told and don't ask questions." I couldn't help but smile when Hettie gave me the stink eye to help her out. "What did his wife say about all of that?"

"She said she didn't know why they dug him up. But the police don't go digging up graves unless they have good evidence." Sugar smacked the bar again. The man could drink beer faster than anyone I had ever seen.

"I heard he was murdered," the bartender said as he pulled the tap putting more beer in Sugar's glass. "At least that was what that fancy reporter said on his way back to Lexington when he stopped in here for a beer."

"Really?" I asked, keeping the questions going.

"Seriously, why are you here?" Chicken stood behind the bar questioning my intentions while he checked out the drinks. "I sure do wish I had a sweet tea. Marla makes the best sweet tea; not that Zula Fae's isn't great, but mmm-mmm, Marla Maria's is pretty good too." Chicken's eyes looked into the air like he was remembering how great it was to be alive. "She loved to come to this old bar. I quit drinking, so she would bring me a jug of sweet tea to sip on while she drank her beers."

I grinned. Memories are all we have and Chicken was living a special one that included Sugar.

"Chicken sat right here." Sugar smacked Hettie's saddle. "That crazy wife of his sat where funeral girl is."

"Emma Lee is my name. 'Funeral girl' is getting a little old." I huffed. "How would you like to be call realtor guy?"

"Add a little Sugar." He kissed the air and blew it my way.

"Ugh." I groaned. "I knew Chicken Teater because he was friends with my daddy. He didn't seem like he would hang out with you."

"I don't know what that means, but Chicken and I did some business dealings years ago and became fast friends." Sugar took a long drink from his glass. He could finish a glass of beer in two big gulps. The bartender set another drink in front of Sugar. My plan was working well. He even let go of Hettie's hand.

"Why were you at his house?" I questioned again, hoping he had forgotten the first time I asked him.

"Lady Cluckington." Sugar took the last of his beer and chugged it. "Sweet Lady. Marla Maria is killing her just like she killed Chicken."

"How so?" Hettie suddenly took a vested interest in what Sugar had to say. She leaned a little closer to Sugar, exposing her chest a little more, making eye candy for him.

"Chicken knew something was going to happen to him." Sugar's eyes narrowed. "He made me promise the week before he died, and he wasn't a bit sick like them doctors in Lexington said he was."

"Made you promise what?" Hettie coaxed him. All I had to do was sit back and listen.

"I promised him I would take great care of Lady and continue to show her at the pageants. One problem," Sugar's eyes closed. He stopped talking. His head bobbled up and down.

"Now what?" Hettie asked me. "He's about to pass out."

"I don't know." I shrugged. "I have to have more. But I don't know what. Just encourage him."

"Gross." Hettie's face contorted. She let out a sigh before she took her hand and reached out to touch Sugar's painted-on hair. "You okay, Sugar?"

"With you I'm doing great," he muttered. Hettie grimaced and her nose curled.

"What do you think about Marla Maria?" she asked in a breathy voice.

"She is a witch. She is slutting around Lexington with Chicken's neighbor and riding all around town in Lady Cluckington's Cadillac. I can't be so sure she didn't kill him and covered it up." Sugar's head nodded. "She even filed for divorce, but Chicken didn't want to lose her so he told her about the property he owned and told her she had to stay with him."

"What property?" Hettie asked.

"Don't worry about that," I said under my breath just enough for her to hear me. I really didn't have to be so discreet, because Sugar was getting loaded by the gulps. "I'll tell you later."

"Did she rip up the divorce papers?" Hettie asked.

"She agreed to take care of Lady if anything happened to him." Sugar threw his hands up in the air. "That's when my buddy died. I miss him so much." Sugar let out a cry and his head came down smacking on the bar top.

"Sugar?" Hettie jabbed him in the arm with her finger. "Sugar?"

"Passed out." The bartender took Sugar's glass and put it behind the bar. "He'll come to soon. Did you get the answers you came to get?"

"What?" Hettie straightened up.

The bartender ran his hand over his mustache and down his mouth before he leaned on the bar with his hands. "I own the place. When I see two girls walk in here all buttoned up and all sudden your junk is hanging out asking all sorts of questions about specific things, I know something is up."

"Did you know Chicken?" I asked.

"I don't know if you are a reporter or not, but I'm not saying a word." The bartender swiped his wet towel on the bar top to clean it off. "But I do know I don't want no trouble around here. You got it?"

"Got it." I grabbed a twenty-dollar bill out of my purse and smacked it on the bar. "It's yours if you tell me how Marla Maria treated Chicken when they were here."

He put his hand on the twenty and eased it closer to him. He slipped it in his jeans' pocket.

"The only thing she talked about was that damn duck—"

"Prize hen," I corrected him.

"What the hell ever. Prize hen." He glared at me. "Do you want your twenty dollars' worth or not?"

"I'm sorry." I put my hands up.

"Anyways, she said that she was going to wring the *prize hen's* neck." He leaned over a little more and whispered, "Chicken said, 'Over my dead body.' Marla Maria said, 'Over your dead body is fine with me.' "

That was as good an admission as I'd ever seen on TV.

"I knew it! I knew she killed me!" Chicken danced on top of the bar. I bit my lip in fear I would laugh out loud. "She's going to pay for this." He jumped down and stared me directly in the eye. "You have to go save Lady Cluckington before Marla kills her too. Then she'll take the money and run!" There was urgency in Chicken's voice. Desperation.

"Thanks," I said to the bartender and grabbed Hettie by the arm, dragging her halfway across the bar.

"I expect you to tell me everything once we get in the car," Hettie warned.

"Wait! Where're you goin'?" Sugar screamed, fumbling words. "Baby!"

We weren't safe from Sugar even outside, safely in the hearse. Sugar stumbled over to the fancy motorcycle with all the lights and tried to throw a leg over like he was going to hop on and follow us, but he couldn't get his five-foot frame up on the seat. He swung a little too hard and fell to the ground.

"Get out of here." Hettie strained her neck to see out of the hearse window.

"No problem." I shifted the gear handle to DRIVE and peeled the hearse wheels out of the gravel parking lot, spitting up pockets of dust. "Damn," I groaned, looking into the rearview. "Charlotte is going to be pissed because the hearse is covered in film."

"You owe me." Hettie draped her arm over the back of the seat. Little did she realize she had positioned her arm perfectly around Chicken's ghost making him scoot a little closer to her and leaving a little bit of room between him and me.

"She sure is a pretty thing." Chicken took in every single facial feature on Hettie Bell's face. "Too bad she wasn't around when I was alive."

I ignored him like I was used to doing.

"Go on. Spill it." Hettie wanted to know why I had dragged her to the Watering Hole. "Plus, I need some hand sanitizer after that goon held my hand." Hettie took her arm off the seat and rubbed it on her capris.

"Awe darlin'," Chicken begged Hettie, "I was just getting used to snugglin' up."

"You know it, and I know there was a reason they had me dig up Chicken Teater." I had to proceed with caution because I couldn't tell her I saw ghosts and the fact we knew Chicken was murdered. "With all the new media I'm sure it will come out." I hesitated.

"You talking about the murder of that man?" Hettie asked. "Remember Zula Fae let it out during yoga." Hettie clasped her hands together and did some sort of breathing exercise. "I have to get my Zen back from that nasty smoky place." Hettie fanned her shirt in and out from her body.

"Regardless." I wasn't going to give in to the

Zen world. I had to go to bed and rest for an early-morning ride to the trailer hood and wait until Marla Maria was out of the house so I could go in and find the agreement and any information about Chicken's doctor. "Doctor!" I hit my palm on the steering wheel.

"What?" Hettie jumped and looked out the window.

"Sugar said something about the doctors and how Chicken wasn't really sick." I tapped the wheel with my finger. "If he wasn't sick, then why did they say he died of pneumonia? And the doctor would have had to sign off on the death certificate because Marla Maria said she called the doctor to come over when Chicken wasn't feeling well. The doctor came to her house and Chicken was dead."

"I don't remember that." Chicken tapped his temple.

"What does that have to do with you? I mean, I get that you date Jack Henry and all, but . . ." Hettie's eyes narrowed. Was she trying to read me?

"Jack Henry is over at Marla Maria's right now. I have to help solve this murder or she's going to try to get her claws into him." I had to admit, playing the girlfriend card was coming in handy.

"Emma Lee Raines, I never pictured you as the jealous type."

"I am." I bit my lip looking over at Chicken Teater and talked to Hettie, but really directed it toward Chicken. "A woman scorned will do anything to get what she wants."

Chapter 11

Hettie Bell was satisfied with my answer of a woman scorned because she didn't make mention of the bar scene the rest of the way home. Apparently, Sugar Wayne didn't make it onto his motorcycle or at least he didn't catch up to us.

"Are you sure you don't want me to go in and check around with you in case there is someone in there?" Hettie asked as we pulled up to Eternal Slumber. Hettie's car was parked at the square from going to the opening ceremony of the Kentucky Festival of Caves.

"No. I'm sure they got what they wanted." I wasn't sure what it was that they wanted, because the only room torn up was Charlotte's office. There was no way they were going to get into the elevator to get Chicken's body or autopsy report.

I glanced over at the funeral home. It was eerily dark. I had never been scared of Eternal Slumber or the contents, but tonight it was a little different. Someone out there killed Chicken. They knew we had dug him up. No thanks to the media, it was obvious Chicken's remains were taken to Eternal Slumber, and the entire state knew we had purchased the new equipment—again, no thanks to the media.

Music spewed from the gazebo in the square. There was a bongo player and guitar player, along with a hippie-looking girl singing her heart out. They weren't on the opening ceremony venue. Apparently, they were visitors taking in the festival while exploring the caves.

"I might just go grab a Diet Coke from one of the food coaches." I pointed to the lively group still gathered at a couple of the scattered picnic tables that the council had put out for the festival.

"I'm going home and taking a long, hot shower." Hettie did a shimmy shake.

I laughed. I didn't blame her. "Did Sugar sprinkle a little too much sugar on you?" I winked.

"Uh." Hettie's tongue protruded out of her mouth as her face scrunched up. "You owe me big time. So be ready to put on a painter's cap. My yoga studio is ready to be painted."

"Sure." I nodded. I'd agree to paint, knowing that once I started she'd ask me to stop since I was so bad with a paintbrush, which was due to my impatience and just slapping it on.

I pulled into Eternal Slumber's driveway and we got out. As we crossed the street, Hettie waved bye on her way to her car and I continued toward the group standing near the beer booth.

"Well, well. How is the star of the show?" O'Dell Burns stood up and stumbled over to the food cart. "You know"—the drink in his cup swashed up and over the rim as he pointed his index finger at me—"it's not good for business to go digging up your clients." He grinned.

"Not here, Mr. Burns." I turned back around to the person working the booth. "I'll have a Diet Coke." I took out some cash from my purse, exchanging it for my drink.

"Why not?" O'Dell slowly rocked from heel to heel. "I think this is a good time," he slurred his words as he held up the sloppy wet cup.

I walked over to the group from where he came. If I would have known he was there, I probably would have gone home and to bed. It was known around the Auxiliary group that O'Dell was a drinker and sometimes took a nip or two while working on a client, making business good for us.

"Hi, Beulah Paige." I nodded when I saw her right in the middle of O'Dell's group. "Does Granny know you are here supporting her competition?"

Where was her loyalty? Beulah Paige would stab you in the back every single time, using her gossiping tongue to do it.

"I didn't realize Zula Fae was on my social calendar." Beulah grinned from ear to ear and looked at each person in the circle of gossipers. She batted her fake lashes at me before she looked at O'Dell. "Isn't that right, O'Dell?"

"That's right." O'Dell stumbled and fell into the spot next to Beulah on the bench. "So, Emma Lee, tell me why you went and dug up poor ol' Chicken?"

"I don't think that is any of your business."

"It is when Marla Maria Teater paid me a visit to rebury her husband after you do God-knows-what to his body." His words stung. Had Marla Maria really contacted Burns Funeral?

Steam poured from my gut and up into my mouth. "I haven't heard from her. Besides, I'm still not going to tell you why."

"As the new mayor of Sleepy Hollow, I promise

here and now . . ." He stood up again, sloshing the contents of his cup all over Beulah's long salt-and-pepper perfectly manicured hair, causing her to jump and shove him to the side, knocking him down. But that didn't stop his loose lips. "I promise here and now that I will never let someone dig up your loved one from their eternal resting place."

"And you think these people are going to elect a town drunk for their mayor?" I shouted at the top of my lungs and gestured to his little group. "And a man who is openly drinking in a public place—not to mention a dry town!"

"Over your crazy granny? I'm a shoo-in with her on the ticket." O'Dell jumped up, coming nose to nose with me. I held my breath. If I took another whiff of the alcohol oozing out of his pores, I just might get drunk from the fumes. "Then you are crazy too. I'm a shoo-in." His lip cocked up to one side.

"Over my dead body!" I balled my fist up and turned on my heels running smack-dab into a kid. "Watch it!"

"You watch it, funeral girl." The kid, who was head and breast to me, was none other than Sugar Wayne. "Where's my girl?"

"Where did you come from?" I asked and noticed the black marks on my shirt from Sugar's dripping hair. In the distance, I could see flashing lights coming around the square and toward the funeral home.

"Watering Hole to claim my babe from you." He jabbed me with his ringed finger. "Oh crap. The po-po."

Sugar Wayne darted into the darkness as fast as his little five-foot frame could carry him.

"Tell my girl I'll find her!" Sugar shouted from the dark abyss.

"You better watch yourself," O'Dell warned. "I'm going to rule this city by taking care of the living and the dead." His grin sent chills over my body.

"Like I said," I glared at him, well aware that Jack Henry's cop car had pulled into Eternal Slumber's driveway. "Over my dead body."

I turned back around and walked across the street to the funeral home wondering why Jack Henry still had the lights of the cruiser on.

"Well, I'd love to bury it." O'Dell's cackle echoed off the hollows of the caves, taunting me over and over until the vibrations stopped.

"Granny?" I watched in shock as Jack Henry opened the back door of the car and removed a handcuffed Zula Fae Raines Payne with a big grin on her face. I took off running to them. "Jack! What are you doing?" I gasped.

"You need to keep a leash on her." Jack whipped Granny around and uncuffed her.

"Where are your manners, Jack Henry Ross?" Granny rubbed each wrist. "Your momma will be getting a call from me."

"Yes ma'am." Jack took his hat off. "Be sure to tell her that I caught you trying to crawl through the window of Burns Funeral Home."

"I'll be." Granny stomped. "I told you he stole my moped."

"Wait." I stood between Granny and Jack Henry, giving them a little distance. I knew Granny and so did Jack. There was no arguing with her. "O'Dell stole your moped?"

Jack Henry let out a big sigh and shook his head.

"He did!" Granny protested. "Ask him!"

"Emma Lee, honey." Jack Henry's slow Southern drawl when he said *honey* sent all reasoning out the window. "Can you please take Zula home?"

"Yes," I muttered, giving him a little smile of gratitude. "I'll be right back."

"I'll wait inside." Jack Henry got in the car and turned off the lights and ignition.

"Come on Granny." I took her by the elbow. "Tell me why you think O'Dell stole your moped."

I made sure to take the back side of the square in fear we would see O'Dell and Beulah. That would send Granny over the edge even further.

"He has it out for me," Granny said in a shaky voice. "He came to the courthouse right after you left and warned me that the first thing on his agenda was to ban mopeds from Sleepy Hollow. He claimed I was going to kill someone." Granny stopped, the moon shone down on her face. There was stress in her eyes. "I'd never hurt a flea. Well, maybe a flea, but not a person."

"I know, Granny." I patted her hand and moved her along. The quicker I got her across to the Inn, the quicker I would be back at my place and looking at Jack Henry. I had to assess him to make sure Marla Maria didn't get her claws into him. "What about the moped?"

"It's gone!" she shrieked. "He left the chain."

"How did he get the chain off?" I asked. The chain was the thickest thing I had ever seen, plus she had a heavy-duty lock on it.

"The key to the lock was on my keys." Granny pouted. "I bet he stole them when he came into the Inn to eat lunch a couple of days ago. That's when I heard him say he was running for mayor.

That's when I decided I had to run against him. Criminal."

"Aren't they all?" I snickered and walked up the steps of the Inn. "Go get some sleep. You are lucky Jack Henry didn't haul you off to jail for breaking and entering. We will talk more in the morning. I'll find the moped."

Granny nodded and disappeared into the Inn.

The crowds had gone from the square and Sleepy Hollow was mostly silent except for the distant bongo drums that echoed throughout the dark night sky.

I had a lot to tell Jack Henry about Marla Maria and why I felt like she killed Chicken.

"Help . . ." The voice gasped for air. "Help me . . ."

"Hello?" I spoke into the dark. The only light was from the carriage lights around the square, which were really there for looks and thus were dim.

"Emma Lee . . ." The voice sounded a lot like O'Dell Burns. My eyes darted to the picnic table where I had left O'Dell gloating. There was a pair of legs sticking out from under the picnic table.

"Help!" I screamed and ran over to him. "Oh-mygod! Ohmygod! Help!" I fell to the ground when I saw blood coming from his side and scooped him into my arms. "It's okay. Jack Henry is right across the street. He will help. Help! Help! Jack Henry!"

"Emma Lee?" Jack Henry appeared on the porch of Eternal Slumber and ran over when he saw me on the ground. He bolted down the stairs screaming something into his police radio. My mind was swirling and everything around me was twirling around.

"It's going to be okay," I whispered to O'Dell rocking him back and forth.

Chapter 12

Sleeping was virtually impossible after the attack on O'Dell Burns and the bags under my eyes were definitely showing it.

I grabbed my notebook off the bedside table and went through the clues I already had because somewhere there had to be a link between O'Dell's attack, Granny's moped theft, and the break-in at the funeral home. Somehow, they had to be connected, and connected to Chicken. But how?

"Chicken has money tied up in property and Marla Maria gets the money based on an agreement where she takes care of Lady Cluckington if something happens to Chicken. Oddly enough, Marla Maria filed for divorce a week before Chicken's supposed pneumonia." I read what I had written. "Marla Maria had the doctor come to her house, where he pronounced Chicken dead from pneumonia."

I grabbed my phone and dialed Vernon Baxter.

"I'm here." Vernon sounded out of breath. "I'm late because of all the news media, but I'm here."

"I didn't know you weren't here. What's up with the news media?" I asked.

"They have the entire town surrounded and are asking everything with two legs about Chicken and his death." I could hear the sound of metal clinking in the background, which meant he was probably working on Chicken's remains with the fancy new tools. "After Jack Henry decided to hold a press conference on the steps of the court-house, the town got crowded."

"He did what?" I gasped and grabbed the remote off the bedside table, flipping the TV on.

"What did you need? The quicker I get the evidence they need, the quicker Sleepy Hollow goes back to being sleepy." Vernon took the words right out of my mouth.

"Did the doctor who pronounced Chicken dead sign the death certificate?" I pinned my phone between my ear and shoulder so I could write down the doctor's name.

"Yes. Let me get his name." Vernon put the

phone down and the shuffling of papers was heard in the background. "Doctor Jeremy Finkel. F-I-N-K-E-L."

"Got it. Thanks." I hit the END button and immediately opened up the browser on my phone searching for Dr. Jeremy Finkel. When his information popped up, I wrote it in the notebook knowing I was going to have to go to Lexington and figure out how to get my hands on Chicken's records.

I flipped back the pages to continue to read what clues I had just in case one of them sparked an idea. "Footprint, see picture on cell phone, feather from Granny's kitchen." I shut the notebook. There was only one way to see where the feather came from and see if Marla Maria owned the shoe that made the print from the kitchen.

"It's about time you got up." Chicken stood near the TV where the camera had focused in on Jack Henry walking to the podium.

"Shh!" I held my finger out to Chicken and pointed to the TV. Using the remote, I turned the volume up on the TV.

"I hope he's going to say he arrested that two-bit—"

"Please." I begged him to be quiet. "I'm trying to listen."

The sound of cameras clicked, making it hard for me to hear Jack Henry's opening remarks. He stepped closer to the plethora of microphones all tied up to the stand in front of him.

"Thank you for coming. I'm Sheriff Jack Henry Ross, here in Sleepy Hollow, Kentucky. I want to assure everyone that Sleepy Hollow is a safe place to visit. We encourage you to come and take part in our semi-annual Kentucky Cave Festival. For your piece of mind, we have added more security. It is true we have opened the case on the death of Colonel C. Teater, based on evidence that he was a victim of a homicide." Jack Henry's deep brown eyes held a serious look I had never seen in them. He meant business. "We are following some very solid leads and asking for the public to come forward if they know of anything that might seem suspicious around the time of Mr. Teater's death four years ago."

The cameras went crazy when Jack Henry took a deep breath.

"As for the attack on Mr. O'Dell Burns last night, we are asking for anyone who saw anything suspicious last night during the opening ceremony of the festival to come forward or call the number on the bottom of your TV screen. We'd like to talk to you. We do not believe the death of Mr. Teater and the attack on Mr. O'Dell are related. Thank you for coming. I will have an update this time tomorrow." Jack Henry stepped away from the media.

Several people yelled out questions. Jack Henry ignored them and got in the cruiser. He flipped the lights on to move the crowd before he took off in the direction of the funeral home.

I jumped up, threw on a pair of jeans, and threw my hair up in a ponytail just in time for a knock at the door.

"I knew you would be over." I opened the door to find Jack Henry leaning up against the frame.

"It's so good to see you." He leaned in and kissed my lips, sending the pit of my stomach into a wild swirl. I angled toward him going deeper into his kiss. "Let's go inside before the cameras follow me here."

"You looked great on TV." I swooned over my celebrity boyfriend. "I'm glad you are here so we can go over some of the clues I have collected along with Chicken's help."

"If it has anything to do with Marla Maria, I'm going to cut you off." Jack Henry stepped up into my efficiency. "I was there most of the night and there was no evidence that she killed Chicken."

"Did her lover come over? Did you see Lady Cluckington? Did you know she filed for divorce a week before Chicken died? And did you know they had an agreement?" I spurted off a lot of questions. His mouth dropped. "Yeah, I'm sure she didn't tell you anything."

I walked past him and walked into the small kitchenette. I stuck a Dunkin' Donuts cup in the Keurig coffeemaker and pushed down, making Jack Henry a cup and then myself one after his was done.

"She didn't say a word about any agreement. She did say they hadn't gotten along right before he got sick." The steam swirled around his face when he took a sip.

"Of course she didn't." My brows lifted. I loved knowing when I was right. "Who is the detective here?" Sarcasm dripped out of my mouth along with the crease of a smile.

"Okay. I admit she did try to flirt, but that was because she was nervous." Jack admitted to Marla Maria trying to get her claws into him.

"Nervous about what?" I knew he would say the media. "No. You have to think like a woman, think like a murderer." I tapped my head. "She was nervous because you were there in her house where your cop instinct was supposed to kick in. And it didn't."

"You are cute trying to be the detective." He pointed around the room. "Is he here?"

"He was. Not now, but I do have some information." I held my finger up and went back to my bedroom to get my notebook.

Jack Henry's phone rang.

"Gotta go!" Jack Henry rushed down the hall. "I'll call you soon. O'Dell Burns is awake from surgery."

I stood at the door with my notebook in my hand and sadly watched as Jack Henry sped toward Lexington, where O'Dell Burns was in the hospital.

"I'm glad he's gone." Chicken stood next to me with his arm loosely draped around my shoulders. I moved away. Though I am comfortable with the whole ghost thing, I was not at all comfortable with the whole touchy thing. "What? He takes you away from the work you are supposed to be doing. Figuring out who murdered me." He puffed his chest out and crossed his arms.

"How does Jack Henry hurt my investigation?" I drank the last sip of coffee in my cup and grabbed my notepad, phone and purse.

"You get all googley inside and your thoughts get filled with all sorts of junk. That is why I get lost. I can't stand all the mushy stuff." Chicken followed closely behind me. "Where are you going? I hope it has something to do with my case."

"I'm going to get a real cup of coffee and then head over to see Marla Maria." I locked the door behind me and Chicken walked right on through it. "You're going to be mad when I tell you this." I took a deep breath and said, "O'Dell told me Marla Maria came to him and she paid him to stick you back in the grave."

"You already stuck me six feet under." There was confusion written on his face.

"The second time around." I twirled my finger around him. We walked down the steps and got in the hearse. Chicken sat right next to me as usual. I was starting to get used to it.

"I wouldn't let O'Dell Burns touch my body and she knows that." Chicken wrapped his arm around my shoulder.

I shimmied in my seat. "Do you have to sit so close?"

"Do you have to take so long to follow up on the leads I'm throwing your way?" He threw a jab back at me.

"I'm not going to break into your trailer. I'm going to go right in and ask Marla Maria about O'Dell and about the agreement." I shifted in my seat and pulled into a space in front of Higher Grounds Café.

Like I was going to talk to him with a crowd watching my every move.

Wait. Why were people watching me?

Chapter 13

"Something weird is going on, Emma Lee." Chicken eased in the door sideways between me and another customer.

"Hi." Cheryl Lynne stood behind the counter of Higher Grounds and wiped her hands down her apron. There were big thermal mugs with steam coming from them and on a table next to her were platters of yummy goodness all ready to be taken over to the square to sell to the festival-goers. She gave a crooked sympathetic smile.

"What is going on?" I asked.

Cheryl Lynne glanced over my shoulder. I turned and followed her line of vision. Beulah Paige, Mable Claire and a couple more of the Auxiliary women stared at me, but quickly turned to their cups of coffee when I looked at them.

"I heard about O'Dell Burns."

"Totally sucks." I peeked at the scones in the glass case standing between us.

"Beulah is going around telling everyone about some sort of altercation you had with him right before someone stuck him with a knife." Cheryl Lynne knew more than I did.

"She what?" I gasped. Thank goodness, my head was attached to my shoulders, because it would have spun right off when I jerked around to look at Beulah. Beulah fidgeted with her strands of pearls draped around her neck and down her chest. I turned back to Cheryl Lynne. "I want a large coffee with light cream. To go."

Nervously Cheryl bit her lip and nodded. "Please don't start something."

"Can you get me a tea?" Chicken asked. I narrowed my eyes, giving him the death look.

"Emma Lee, what are you looking at?" Cheryl didn't miss a thing. She obviously saw me glare at Chicken, only to her it looked like I was glaring into the air. "Do you need to see Doc Clyde about the Funeral Trauma? Because Beulah said you might be—"

"Geez!" I stopped her right there. "Coffee,

Cheryl," I ordered and smacked a couple of dollars on the glass counter before I turned to face Beulah.

"Good morning, Emma Lee." Beulah tilted her head to the side and peered down at her cup. She pursed her lips.

"Beulah Paige Bellefry, don't you go around and good morning me when you are spreading gossip like wildfire. You know good and well that I didn't hurt O'Dell Burns." I planted my hands on my hips. Chicken stood on the other side of her with his hands planted on his hips.

"I didn't say any such thing." She gave a quick shake of her head and put her chin in the air before she straightened her back, making her sit very tall. "I only told people about Marla Maria Teater paying O'Dell Burns a visit about reburying her late husband. Rest his soul." Beulah made the sign of the cross. The Auxiliary women gave an "amen" in unison.

"You aren't even Catholic." I glared at her. "Shame on you and you and you." I pointed to the women sitting around the gossip table. "From now on, you worry about yourselves and leave me out of it."

"She's as windy as a bag full of farts," Chicken said as serious as could be.

I busted out laughing. I tried to stop, but it wasn't going to happen. Even Chicken let out a little giggle.

"See, she's crazy." Beulah nodded to all the women. "Ever since that plastic Santa fell off Artie's roof and hit her square in the head, she ain't been right."

She picked up her cup and tipped it up to her mouth to take a drink. Chicken reached out and plucked the bottom of the cup making Beulah tip it a little too much, spilling the hot liquid all down her fancy pearls and into her lap.

"See?" I pointed to the sky. "Gossip is a sin." Pleased as pie, I grinned and trotted over to the counter to get my coffee.

Leaving Higher Grounds, I could see Beulah glaring at me in my peripheral vision as the other women fell over each other to dab at Beulah's blouse.

"That was great." Chicken skipped to the car, swinging his arms. "She deserves that and more. Now where to?"

We got back into the hearse. Chicken got in his normal position—next to me. I shrugged. He didn't notice.

"We are going to your house." I started the

hearse and pulled out, making sure I didn't hit anyone.

The square was filling up fast. The food booths were open and smoke was coming from the barrels of bonfires set throughout the square. It took a couple of hours for the fog and brisk morning air to roll away from the hollow. The fire pits added a nice touch to the festival, making it more cozy and enjoyable.

Within minutes, Chicken and I were sitting in the hearse in front of his double-wide, staring at it through the window. Neither of us said a word for about a minute.

"I hope she lets you in," Chicken said softly.

I took a deep breath and got out of the hearse, making sure I locked it.

"You sure could have fixed these steps." Cautiously, I climbed up the three makeshift steps to the door of the trailer and tapped on the door.

The front porch light came on and the door swooped open. Marla Maria wore a long black housedress with a tight black tank top and black leggings. Leopard print heels made her taller and thinner than she already was. Her hair was pinned all over her head.

She patted her head and started to take out all

the bobby pins. "I wasn't expecting company. Of all people, not you. Please excuse my hair. I haven't fixed it yet because I have my bi-weekly appointment at Girl's Best Friend today."

Oh crap! I had totally forgotten I had an appointment with Mary Anna today. I ran my fingers through my hair.

"I wanted to speak with you about something. May I come in?" I asked.

She hesitated.

"You have to compliment her." Chicken stood next to her and took a big whiff of her hair. "She always smelled so good."

"I can't believe you are going to get your hair done." I pushed my fingers in mine to puff out my hair. "It looks great to me."

"Come on in." She didn't look like she was convinced that I had given her a compliment.

"Telling her she's pretty works every single time." Chicken smiled like he knew exactly what he was doing.

I stepped inside. The wood paneling made the room look very dark. There were a couple of fabric-covered La-Z-Boys, each with an afghan draped over the arm. The kitchen was small, and steam was rolling from four pots on the stove. The hardwood flooring was as shiny as a new penny.

There wasn't a feather or piece of chicken dander anywhere to be seen. Not that I didn't think Marla Maria was a good housekeeper, I just figured she didn't bother with it because it seemed a little beneath her.

"What do you want?" Delicately she walked over to the stove while putting on an apron covered with chicken pictures, picked up a ladle and stirred whatever was in the big stockpot. "I'm in a hurry."

"I've heard some rumblings around town."

"You mean O'Dell Burns spread his lips?" She shook her head. "Yep. I told him to keep it on the down-low but when I heard he was running for mayor against Zula Fae Raines Payne, I knew he was going to use it to his advantage." She shook the ladle toward me. A little something flung off it and flew past my shoulder. "O'Dell is slicker than pig snot on a radiator." She turned back around and continued to stir.

"Whoo-weeee!" Chicken smacked his leg. "She's making Lady Cluckington her favorite meal."

"I just think it's best that I cut ties with Eternal Slumber. Nothing against you, Emma Lee," Marla said, but I wasn't so sure she was telling the truth.

"Marla Maria, I was only doing what the police

told me to do." I stated the facts but left out the parts where I believed she was the one who killed Chicken and the reason they dug him up. I didn't think she would like that.

"I just don't get why they think he was murdered." She shook her head. "He was a saint." She dabbed the corner of her eye.

Chicken started clapping. "And the Academy Award goes to Marla Maria Teater." He clapped so loud it made my ears ring. "I don't care who puts me back in the grave as long as you put her in jail. Go on and ask her about the food."

"I didn't know you were a chef." I used the word *chef* loosely.

"Chef? You mean slave to that . . . that," Marla Maria raised her forearm and wiped some steam off her brow. "I mean, sweet Lady Cluckington is on a special diet. On Chicken's deathbed, I promised him I would take extra great care of her."

"You mean you killed me because you wanted to get your hands on my half a million!" He spat on the floor near her feet. *If only it weren't ghost spit*, I sighed.

"I have to go up to Lexington to that fancy whole food store and buy all sorts of things to feed her." Marla Maria pulled out a piece of paper from her apron pocket and read from it. "Kelp granules, millet, oat groats, black oil sunflower seeds, hard red wheat berries, kamut, whole corn kernels, brewer's yeast." She put the list to her chest. There was a disgusted look on her face. "Have you ever heard of such ingredients?"

"No," I whispered.

"Those are the things I have to go buy once a week in order to take care of our precious Lady." There was a monotone in her voice.

"But isn't she a chicken?" I asked. I had to play off the fact that I knew that Lady and she didn't get along. Rephrase—that she didn't like Lady.

"You'd better be glad Chicken is dead or he would have a fit hearing you say that." She laughed. The lines at the edges of her eyes deepened, creating a glow on her face. "He would be madder than a wet hen if he heard you say that. Speaking of wet hen," she grabbed a pot off the stove, "I've got to go feed Lady, so if you'd like to meet her come along."

"Get a glass of that sweet tea." Chicken stood next to the stove and pointed to the pitcher of sun tea sitting on the windowsill. "Marla Maria might not be the best at making Lady Cluckington's food, but she does give Zula Fae a run for her money in the tea department." Chicken licked his lips. "Mmm-mmm. Sweet and sugary."

"I'd love to." I tried to keep my voice steady and my eyes on her, but Chicken made it difficult as he danced around Marla doing his best chicken impression and acting like he was going to peck her in the neck.

"*Bock, bock.* Open the cabinet door under the TV." Chicken strutted over to the family room and scratched his foot at a door in the entertainment center like a chicken scratching at the dirt.

I glared at him. How did he expect me to open the door when Marla Maria was right there? What was in there anyway?

"Open the door!" Chicken protested when Marla Maria and I walked past it.

My mind reeled trying to think how I could get away from her and see what Chicken wanted me to see.

"You comin'?" Marla Maria asked and held the back screen door open.

"Uh . . . yes." I smiled and followed her out the back door.

The fenced-in backyard was very charming. There was a small garden to the left of the yard and on the right side was the chicken coop, which looked like a mini-mansion. The two-story white colonial structure was nicer than the trailer. No wonder Marla Maria was jealous. I could see why. It seemed that Chicken took better care of Lady than he did Marla Maria.

"Lady C! *Cluck, cluck, cluck.*" Marla Maria clicked her tongue on her teeth and banged the ladle on the pot.

"Lady girl! Lady girl!" Chicken shouted from the top of his ghostly lungs.

A dust ball exploded from the lettuce patch in the garden. Within seconds, a low-flying chicken darted out. The red-and-white feathered creature was a dirty mess. She pecked at the ground around Chicken Teater's feet and would look up as if she knew he was there.

"That's my sweet Lady." Chicken bent down and touched her. She bent her head up to the sky.

"What is that crazy thing doing?" Marla Maria watched Lady Cluckington shift right and left as if she was being petted. And she was, only Marla Maria couldn't see Chicken Teater and Lady Cluckington reuniting.

"She sees me!" Chicken looked up. There were tears streaming down his face. "And she's a dirty mess." He glared at Marla Maria. "But she's gotten fat, so that means Marla has been feeding her."

"Why is she so dirty?" I asked and tried to

ignore the unusual behavior Lady Cluckington displayed. I had heard animals had a sixth sense of seeing beyond the living.

"The darn thing loves to take dirt baths. Chicken would die. But she is happy and she loves it." Marla Maria walked over to the coop and unlocked the chicken wire gate. "Come on Lady." Frustration had settled on Marla Maria's face.

"Why do you keep it locked if you let her run around?" Moving Marla Maria's concentration away from Lady Cluckington was proving difficult as she continued to peck around Chicken Teater. It did look like Lady was going a little cuckoo, pecking while darting around in a circle.

"She misses me so much." Chicken popped a squat in the dirt and let Lady jump in his lap.

"I think she's losing it." Marla Maria could only see Lady jumping up and down in the dirt. If she could only see how happy Chicken Teater looked. "Come on, you crazy-assed bird!" Marla Maria screamed, causing Lady and Chicken both to jump.

Lady did what she was told and darted off through the open gate. Marla Maria practically threw the homemade slop on the ground before she locked Lady in.

"She can stay in there all night for all I care." Marla Maria jerked her heel out of the mud. "Look what you did to my new heels." Marla Maria huffed off in the direction of the trailer, and I quietly followed behind, trying to devise a new game plan in my head.

"Emma Lee," Chicken ran beside me with his hands out, "you can't let her leave Lady in there."

In the background, Lady was clucking and bocking up a storm. Without looking, I could hear her wings flapping in distress. The further away Chicken Teater got from Lady, the more Lady made a ruckus.

"She's going to hurt herself!" Chicken pleaded.

"Do you think you should check on Lady?" I asked Marla Maria before we walked back in the trailer.

"Really? Did Chicken possess your body or something?" She turned and glared at me before she shoved me to the side and marched back over to the coop.

"Something like that," I muttered under my breath and opened the trailer door. "I'll be inside waiting on you."

I didn't give her time to respond before I hurried back to the TV entertainment center and opened the door Chicken had begged me to open.

"Chicken?" I called out and bent down to see what was in there. "Help me," I whispered.

The only thing in there was a stack of magazines. *Cock and Feathers* magazines to be exact.

"You wanted me to look in here, so help me." I glanced around the room to see if he was there.

"Hurry! She's coming back in." Chicken gestured me to hurry. "Grab the magazines. You need the magazines."

"And how do I do that?" I quietly shut the door back when I heard Marla Maria's heels coming up to the back door. I stood up.

"I have no idea what is going on with that crazy hen, but I do know I can't wait until I can get out of here." Marla Maria eyed me. "What were you doing in here?"

"I . . . I . . ." I stuttered and picked up a brochure that was sitting on the entertainment center next to the TV. "I was looking at your brochure."

Marla Maria's demeanor did a complete turnaround. She clapped her hands together and bolted toward me, wrapping my hands in hers.

She darted her head back and forth. Her eyes scanned me up and down.

"I'd never taken you for a beauty queen, but you

might have what it takes." She brushed my hair with her fingernails. "You do have some sort of underlying beauty no matter what Chicken did say about you."

"What did he say?" I glanced over her shoulder and darted a glare toward Chicken. He was fidgety, as he should've been. I rolled one eyebrow up when I caught his attention.

"He always said Charlotte was the prettier of you two. You know he was good friends with your daddy." Marla Maria continued to put my hair up in all sorts of makeshift updos. "But you have a natural beauty, and judges love that. Especially at your age."

"I didn't say I wanted to be a beauty queen."

"What about the Orloff Queen?" Chicken nodded ferociously.

"Then why were you so interested in my brochure?" Marla Maria cocked her head. "I'm planning on opening a beauty school where I teach girls how to walk, talk, eat and be queens."

I looked at the brochure in my hand and read the first line, "Marla Maria's School of Beauty." My mouth formed an *O*. "Beauty Queen School for all ages?" I read the tagline.

"Yes." Marla Maria snatched the brochure out

of my hands. "There are pageants all over the world for all ages."

"Orloff Queen!" Chicken stomped his feet. "There is an Orloff Queen at the state pageant, which is tomorrow."

"Tomorrow?" I spouted aloud and clamped my mouth when I realized what I had done.

"Tomorrow is the pageant for the state Orloff competition." She tapped her chin before her long red fingernail, looking more like a dagger, came toward my face and made a swirly around my brows. "How did you know about the pageant?"

"I read an issue of *Cock and Feather* magazine at Doc Clyde's place and instantly thought about you and how respected you are in the pageant community." If she loved compliments, I was going to give them to her. "But I'm sure it's too late for me to enter the beauty pageant."

"It's a little fair pageant." She dropped her claws from my face and clasped them in front of her. "You can enter as soon as you get there. But we can't have you going like that." She twirled her finger in front of my face. "Maybe you should take my spot in the chair at Girl's Best Friend."

"I have an appointment today." I couldn't believe I was about to agree to do a chicken pageant when I knew nothing about chickens. Not to mention putting myself in danger of being in the presence of a killer. At least I was getting somewhere when the police department was getting nowhere. "But I only wish I could get my hands on some of the *Cock and Feather* magazines."

"Oh honey," Marla Maria's hand swiped the air. "I've got plenty down there in that cabinet." She pointed to the door underneath the TV. "Help yourself."

"Hot damn!" Chicken screamed. "Take them all and hold them from the bottom."

"Great!" I bent down and opened the cabinet. I did exactly what Chicken had told me to do and held the heavy stack of magazines close to me. "I'll look through them and prepare myself before tomorrow."

"That is thinking like a real winner." Marla Maria draped her arm around my shoulder and opened the brochure with the other hand. "Chicken has this little piece of property in Lexington that I will inherit when Lady dies, and I'm going to open up a fancy pageant school there. Right now I rent a spot underneath my brother's doctor's office."

"Beauty-pageant school." Chicken shuffled his feet. "Stupidest thing I have ever heard and I told her that too."

"Your brother is a doctor?" I asked and peeled myself from underneath her arm. A beauty pageant school might be one of the stupidest things he had ever heard of but it was a motive to get her hands on the property. People did weird things to make their dreams come true. Marla Maria was no different.

"Oh yeah." Marla Maria sashayed to the kitchen. She opened the freezer and took out some ice cubes to put in a glass before she poured some tea into it. Chicken stood next to her with envy in his eyes. "Jeremy is the smart one and I'm the pretty one." She winked and took a long drink.

Jeremy? My mind rolled back to my conversation with Vernon. Doctor Jeremy Finkel was the doctor who signed off on Chicken's death certificate.

I hugged the magazines tighter to my chest as the lump of "oh crap" made its way to the pit of my stomach. Of course, the doctor was part of this whole grand scheme.

I could just see it now. Marla Maria filed for divorce before she knew about the property. Chicken begged her to stay by giving her the agreement. With Chicken out of the way, Marla Maria could slowly neglect Lady Cluckington and she'd die. That would leave Marla Maria free reign of the property to build her dream of owning and operating a beauty-pageant school and no one would ever suspect she killed him. Certainly, her brother wasn't going to turn her in. I would put money on it that he was getting some sort of payback from her pageant school.

"Anyway, you need to go so I can get to my appointment with Mary Anna Hardy." She put her hands on my shoulders and steered me toward the door. "I'll tell her what I want her to do with your brows and hair. You meet me here tomorrow morning at 6 A.M. We have to get on the road. I'll have an outfit for you."

She stepped back and looked me over from head to toe. She gestured for me to turn around. I twirled.

She rubbed her chin. "Are you a size six?" I nodded. "Goody! I just might bring home two beauty queens tomorrow!" There was way too much excitement in her voice. "See you in the morning."

I left without saying anything to her because I was speechless. The killer was right here and I had to tell Jack Henry.

Chapter 14

Jack, you have to call me as soon as you get this message." I knew he was with a half-out-of-it O'Dell Burns, which I'm sure was painful for Jack Henry. O'Dell was difficult to be around when he hadn't been a victim of a murderer, so I couldn't imagine how he would be, knowing he had been a target and lived. "See if O'Dell has any pre-need funeral information." I chuckled. "Okay, that might have been bad form." I probably shouldn't have made a joke, but it was too good to resist. Just because he had been stabbed didn't mean there was going to be a truce to our long-standing family feud. "I have to give you some very important information. The doctor who signed off on Chicken Teater's death cer—"

Beep. Beep.

I pulled the phone away from my ear. It had died and I didn't have a charger to plug it into. I threw it in the passenger seat just in time for Chicken to appear next to me in his usual spot with his arm draped over my shoulder.

"I can't wait to see you all dolled up as a beauty queen." He laughed. "She will have you looking just like her."

"Apparently, you don't think I'm as pretty as Charlotte." Questioning him about the doctor was more important, but I was still a girl, and my feelings were hurt. Especially since I was the one helping him, not Charlotte.

"Oh, you can't believe everything Marla Maria tells you," he quipped.

"I can't?" I questioned. "If that is the case, then you need to go right back up to the big guy," I pointed to the sky, "and maybe he is the reason you can't cross over."

Cough, cough. Chicken covered his mouth as if he were choking on his own spit. "Okay. Fine. I might have said something about Charlotte. But you have grown into your own." He nodded.

"I don't know what that means. So I'm going to concentrate on getting you to the other side and

I think Marla and Jeremy are in on it." I glanced over at the magazines I had stuck on the floorboard. "What's with those anyway?"

"You have to pick up the first three copies," he said.

At the next stoplight before the town square, I bent down and did what he told me to do. Underneath the first three issues, he had glued the rest together and cut a hole in the middle big enough for some old VHS tapes.

"There are three videotapes in there from me videotaping everything going on around my house the week before I died. There has to be something on there to help us peg Marla Maria for sure."

"I believe Marla Maria is deep into your death like she is in makeup, but she's taking care of Lady and putting her in the pageant along with me tomorrow, and holding up her end of the agreement." I smacked my hand on the wheel. "I forgot to ask about the agreement."

"Marla Maria has a way of turning on the charm and making people forget all sorts of things." He grinned. "I think you lost your marbles agreeing to be in the Orloff pageant."

"I must have." I looked down at the tapes again

before the light turned green. "Granny has one of those old tape players and I need to see her anyway."

I turned the hearse down the street that ran alongside the square near the Inn and pulled into the gravel lot for Inn customers only. There were a lot people on the Inn's front porch enjoying the local bluegrass band playing in the gazebo across the street. They didn't pay any attention to the big flashing sign in the Inn's yard with Granny's picture printed on it telling people to vote for Zula Fae Raines Payne for Mayor. Mable Claire and Beulah were passing out some sort of button to people walking by. Little did they realize, half the people they were targeting weren't even Sleepy Hollow residents. They didn't care. As long as their lips were moving, they were happy.

"Get in here." Granny rushed me through the front door of the Inn and back to the kitchen, where she had a big pot of chili on the stove. "What's in your hand?"

"I wanted to know if I could use that old VHS tape player of yours to watch some of these old tapes I found." I held them tight in fear Granny would grab one and take off with it.

"Sure." Granny poured me a glass of iced tea and gestured for me to sit at the old farm table. I did what she wanted and waited to see what she had to say. I could tell she was about to explode by how fast she stirred the chili. "You have got to stop going around and threatening people. Beulah was trying to get close to O'Dell so she could get in Burns Funeral to find my moped. We were going to expose him for being a thief. Who would want a thief as their mayor?"

Granny posed a good question.

"Granny, how was I to know? You know I don't like anyone talking about my family. Especially O'Dell Burns." I picked up the tea and took a long sip. Chicken appeared next to me.

"I just want a sip." He licked his lips.

"You were the one that was caught breaking and entering at his place and slandering him for saying he was going to ban scooters." I stated the facts. Facts were facts when it came to crimes. That was why it was important for me to see what was on the tapes.

"What are you two doing?" Jack Henry stood at the kitchen door. He looked so handsome in his uniform. His dark eyes made my heart melt.

"We are talking about getting a bowl of chili." Granny gave me the stink eye. I knew not to tell him what we were really talking about until she left the room. Then I'd spill my guts.

"Did you get my message?" I asked. "You need to check out the doctor who signed off on the death certificate." I winked.

"Why are you getting involved in Chicken Teater's death?" Granny asked and looked between us. "You better not be using my granddaughter for any sort of police work because she is not trained to do that. She is a certified mortician."

The word *mortician* gave me the heebies. I'd much rather be called an undertaker.

"I'll call you later." Jack Henry's eyes met mine and then slid to Granny. "Zula, can you come down to the station to answer a few questions about your whereabouts last night? I also need to talk to you about trying to get into Burns Funeral Home."

"Here we go again." Granny held her wrists out in front of her. This wasn't her first time going down to the Sleepy Hollow police department to answer questions about a murder. "Emma Lee was here last night when O'Dell was attacked. Ask her."

"I know that is what you two said, but I have to get a formal statement." He reached out and touched Granny. "I'm not going to cuff you. Just come quietly and you will be back soon."

Granny and Jack Henry walked toward the door. Jack Henry turned around.

"I will follow up on that lead. Thank you." He winked back. It was hard for me to get mad at him for questioning a little old lady, although Granny was far from acting old, but I knew it was his job. "And dinner . . ." he hesitated.

"Don't worry." I smiled, knowing he was about to cancel. "I know you have a lot of investigating to do. I'll text you." That was our signal for him to know I had some information he might need. I actually had a lot of information, but some of it was speculation and I knew he wouldn't follow a lead on speculation. Jeremy and Marla Maria were siblings. There was no speculation on that. It was probably a good place for him to start.

"And that tape player is in my bedroom." Granny nodded. "I'll be back soon."

I smiled, knowing she'd be back soon because she hadn't touched O'Dell Burns, even though we both had dreamed of it.

The clock on the kitchen wall said I had just enough time to pop in one of the tapes before my hair appointment with Mary Anna at Girl's Best Friend Spa. I could see what I was dealing with and while Mary Anna was doing my hair, I could try to concentrate on my game plan just in case Jack Henry hadn't solved the crime by the time the pageant rolled around.

After making my way up the steps to Granny's room at the Inn, I shut the door behind me. Chicken had already beaten me up the stairs and was sitting comfortably in Granny's lounger.

"Ready for the show?" Chicken rubbed his hands together in delight.

"I guess." I fiddled with a few buttons on the old TV that had the built-in VHS player. It had been a very long time since I had touched this thing. I popped the tape in and immediately it started to play.

I stepped back and eased myself onto Granny's bed, never taking my eyes off the screen. Marla Maria darted around the house while Chicken stayed in his comfy chair, Lady Cluckington sitting next to him.

"She's a beaut." He referred to Lady every time she was in the picture.

I had to admit, Lady was much cleaner when Chicken was alive. Her red and white feathers were spotless.

"Red and white feathers?" I stood up and hit the PAUSE button. "Lady Cluckington has red and white feathers. Not a streak of gold in them."

"Wow! You can see." Chicken said with a smart-aleck tone.

"The feather we found in Granny's kitchen is streaked with gold and black. There isn't a speck of red on it." I paced back and forth. "That means that someone else is involved."

"And not Marla Maria?" Chicken asked with a hopeful tone in his voice.

I bit my lip. "I really thought I had this thing figured out. But what if there was someone at the pageants that wanted to knock you off the winner's block? Someone with a gold-and-black chicken?"

"I don't recall an Orloff with gold in it." Chicken shook his head. "Marla Maria killed me. Look at her." He shoved his hand toward the TV.

I pushed PLAY. He was right. Marla Maria showed her distaste for Lady Cluckington but I couldn't be so sure she killed Chicken.

"What about Jeremy and all that?" Chicken began to protest. He spouted off everything we had already dug up. "What about the agreement? You even said it was a good motive."

"But would the real killer try to pin all the evidence on Marla Maria to get the heat off their own back?" I didn't know if I truly believed what I was saying, but it sounded like something out of *CSI* and it sounded pretty darn good.

"What are you going to do about it?" Chicken asked.

"Well, I'm going to go get my hair done." I bit at my nails and took the cassette out of the player. The others were going to have to wait, because it was time to get my hair all fluffed up for my beauty-queen debut. "Then I'm going to do the pageant tomorrow and see if there is anyone suspicious around. If someone wanted to kill you, then maybe they will be there."

I knew it was a long shot but it was all I had. Marla Maria was still the prime suspect and she hadn't let Lady Cluckington be shown at any fairs over the last couple of years. I had a feeling that I was about to find out all sorts of answers to my questions come pageant time.

Chapter 15

"There she is," Mary Anna sang from the top of her lungs from behind her client's head when I walked into Girl's Best Friend Spa, "Miss Chicken Queen." This was followed by a roomful of applause coming from women underneath the dryers and in the styling chairs.

I did my best princess wave before I bent down into a full curtsey only to land square on my butt.

"Ouch." I got up and rubbed out the sting on my hind end. "Word spreads fast around here." I took a seat in the waiting lounge near the front door until it was my turn.

"I never figured you for the beauty-queen type." Mary Anna planted her hand on her hip, the scissors still attached to her finger and thumb as she leaned to one side. She went back to cutting the woman's hair who was in the chair. "Ever since I cut and colored your hair a few months ago, you haven't looked back."

I laughed. I wanted to tell them the truth, but it would come out soon enough. Truth be known, I was more confused now than I was when they dug up Chicken's casket. The golden feather had me thrown off, even though there was sufficient evidence against Marla Maria in my opinion. But opinions didn't matter in real-life investigations according to Jack Henry.

"Well come on." Mary Anna pushed her boobs back into her too-tight scoop-neck top and stuck the tip from her last client deep within her cleavage. "I've got to get you in pageant condition according to Marla Maria Teater."

"What exactly does that mean?" I asked. A little worry stuck in my gut made me a tad bit nauseous.

"Don't you worry. If you want to win, you just let me work my magic." Mary Anna did a little shimmy shake in her short pencil skirt before she looked in the mirror and grabbed a comb to tease up her bangs. "Higher to God, girl. Higher to God."

Patiently, I waited for Mary Anna to come back from wherever she disappeared to, taking in all the women in the salon and trying to figure out how I was going to bring up Chicken and start some gossip about Marla Maria. I didn't have to wait too long.

"Honey, aren't you a little old to be in a beauty pageant?" A little old lady leaned over from the drying chair and asked.

"Excuse me?" Feeling a little offended, I wanted some clarification.

"You have to be in your twenties." The woman's beady little eyes stared me down.

"There are many types of pageants nowadays." Another woman chimed in. "They have Mrs. America too." She nodded her head. They started talking amongst themselves. I was too busy watching Mary Anna mix up some sort of concoction in front of me at the station where all her styling tools were displayed.

"I'm really excited about this." Exuberance dripped from her face. The more she stirred the stuff in the bowl, the bigger her smile grew. "I never dared to dream you would go for it. When Marla Maria told me what to do to you, I started salivating!"

Salivating? I swallowed the lump in my throat. I didn't dare protest or even ask what she had in store for me.

"Can I ask one favor?" I used my tiptoes to turn the salon chair around. "Can you please not show me the results until the end?"

Mary Anna was all too accommodating. She tugged, pulled, clipped, painted, and put stuff on my hair that I couldn't imagine what it was for. She grabbed a big roll brush and hair dryer, nearly scorching my scalp because it was so hot. The tugging to the sky made me think about the Miss America pageants I used to watch on TV. To clarify—I didn't turn them on—Charlotte did.

"Okay." Mary Anna turned the hair dryer off. She pushed a button with her foot, sending me straight back in the chair. She took a small brush and combed through my eyebrows. "I've been dying to get my hands on these." Fear knotted in my stomach. I truly thought I was going to barf as Mary Anna took a small wooden stick out of the melted wax and rolled it around before telling me to close my eyes.

"Ouch!" My eyebrows felt like they were being burned off my face. "That hurts!"

"Honey, that's nothin'."

Rip!

"Holy . . ." I screamed a few expletives that would have made my Granny blush as Mary Anna ripped the wax off my face. I felt like a plucked chicken. I threw my hands up to my face. "Did you rip off all of my brows?" I jumped up and looked in the mirror. "What in the . . ." A few more expletives came out, making me feel like I needed to wash my own mouth out with soap.

"You have very thin skin." Worry spread across Mary Anna's face as she stood behind me looking in the mirror at my reflection.

The only thing I recognized in the mirror were my eyes, and the only real reason I knew they were mine was because they were staring back at me. Long gone was my brown hair, which was now bleached blond, and my brows had disappeared into the swollen red patches above my eyes.

"What have you done to me?" I asked through gritted teeth before I burst out crying. I fell back into the chair with my head planted in my hands.

"I . . ." Mary Anna Hardy didn't know what to say. Her mouth dropped open and clamped shut a few times before something finally came out. "I'm doing what your pageant coach told me to do. You are the one who didn't protest. Please don't be mad, Emma Lee."

"What's wrong with you? Don't you be going

and gettin' too big for your britches," Chicken said. With my head still planted in my hands, I could see Chicken's bare feet through the crack of my fingers. "You have a job to do. It's hair. It can be dyed back after the pageant. Now, where are your manners? You are a Southern girl who is going to win that pageant and figure out who killed me."

Sniff, sniff. Chicken was right. It was only hair, and I needed to play the part in order to figure out who killed him so he could have everlasting peace.

"Marla Maria did say that making Emma Lee look like a beauty queen would be a long shot," one of the other stylists whispered loud enough for me to hear. "She even said she was going to bring out the Cadillac so the pageant judges would see Emma Lee arrive in style and think she was from old money or something."

The more I heard, the madder I got. Not only was I going to show Marla Maria that I was going to be an awesome Orloff Queen, I was going to show her how well this queen was going to solve the murder that she committed.

Slowly, I lifted my head. Mary Anna held her hands up to her face as if she thought I was going to come up swinging. I straightened my shoulders and shook my new bleached blond hair behind my shoulders.

"I'm going to be the next Orloff Beauty Queen in Kentucky." I stood up and gave a princess wave. All eyes were on me. "Then I'm going to go over to the square and represent Sleepy Hollow in the Kentucky Cave Festival."

"That's my girl." Chicken rubbed his hands together before wiping the sweat that was dripping down the side of his face. "It's hotter than a Billy goat's ass in a pepper patch with all this gossip going on. Let's get out of here."

"Thank you, Mary Anna." I smiled and raised my hands up to my nonexistent brows. "Ouch." I grimaced.

Of course she didn't want me to be mad. I was her employer in the after-death world of hairdressing. God knew why Mary Anna Hardy loved to do hair for the dead, but she did.

Chapter 16

She plucked you like a chicken for that beauty pageant." Chicken stood behind me and stared into the mirror at my wet hair. "And I wouldn't put it past Marla Maria to have planned for you to turn out that way."

As soon as I left Girl's Best Friend, I rushed home and took a shower using extra, extra shampoo and conditioner in hopes the blond dye would wash out. But that was wishful hoping. In fact, it looked a lot lighter than before.

"I'll show her." I glared at him, and then picked up the brush. I racked it through my hair and used the curling brush like I had seen Charlotte do when we were growing up.

The loose curls hung nicely around my face.

The soft blond color gave my olive complexion a nice glow. It was strange seeing what the change of hair color could do. It made me look like a completely different person.

The knock at the door caused me to jump. I tucked the loose strands of hair behind my ears and walked to the door. Through the peephole, I could see Jack Henry standing with a small bouquet of flowers in his hands.

"I've been trying to call you all day." He held the flowers up, covering his face. "I'm sorry about missing our dates." He dropped the flowers to his side. His big smile froze, then his lips turned down and dropped open. "Emma Lee?"

"Oh!" I had forgotten my phone was in the hearse. Dead. I smacked my palm on my forehead, catching a little bit of the swollen brow. Jack Henry had yet to see the new hair color. "Ouch!" I winced in pain.

"What happened to your eyebrows?" he asked.

"And my hair?" I questioned him before I burst into tears for the fourth time since Mary Anna had turned me into a stripper.

"I've never dated a blonde before." He swept me into his arms. "It's only hair." He held me close to his chest as I heaved in and out.

It took me years to finally get Jack Henry to

notice me and become my boyfriend. I didn't want my amateur investigating to hinder any of it, but he seemed to be understanding of the hair color. I had yet to tell him why I had changed it.

I molded myself against him wanting a little more attention. It had been a few long days without cuddling with him. I looked up into his deep brown eyes. I lifted my hand and rubbed the edge of his hairline. He bent down. His lips found mine. The sweet throbbing of his lips made me shift even closer to him.

"Not that your hair looks bad . . ." Jack Henry's lips found my forehead. They deepened into a smile. He was cautious with his words. His momma taught him well. " . . . but why did you decide to go blond?"

His lips seared down my neck, planting tantalizing kisses in the hollows of my collarbone.

Did my blond hair have this effect on him? My brown hair certainly didn't. Was this the moment I had been waiting for? My mind wouldn't shut up long enough for me to enjoy his roaming hands and hot lips.

"Emma Lee." His breath was hot against my ear. "You are driving me crazy. Tell me why you decided to be blond? Were you trying to spice things up?"

I slightly pulled away, still feeling his heartbeat.

"You aren't going to like my answer." It was time to come clean. I was regretting changing my appearance to help solve a case based on circumstantial evidence.

His mouth clenched. "I guess you better tell me," his voice hardened. He stepped inside and followed me to the little sitting area in my efficiency.

He sat down next to me on the love seat. I took his hands in mine. He was not going to be happy.

"Please let me finish before you go off on me." I swallowed hard. "You know I can't just let clues that Chicken Teater tells me sit around while you do the cop thing, which I know is the right thing, but . . ." I put my hands in the air in a sort of truce way. " . . . I have sufficient clues to make me certain Marla Maria killed Chicken Teater."

Jack Henry let go of my hands. He shifted, finally resting his hands between his knees.

"Marla Maria had filed for divorce one week"—I held my finger up for dramatics—"before Chicken died. Chicken begged her to stay and offered her an agreement."

"An agreement?" Jack Henry rolled his eyes, sort of pissing me off.

"Why is that hard to believe?" I stood up to face

him, but didn't look at him directly. "Hear me out. The agreement says Marla Maria can have all of Chicken's money, including the property he owns that is worth over half a million dollars."

"Chicken Teater lived in a double-wide. Don't you think he would have moved up into something else if he had half a million?"

"What's wrong with a double-wide?" I asked. He didn't know my parents lived in Sleepy Hollow Park when I was a little girl before we moved into the funeral home. I shook my head, refusing to get off the subject. "Anyway, he does. You can check the courthouse records. The agreement says she has to stay married to him and if anything happens to him she has to take care of Lady Cluckington."

"The chicken?" Jack Henry bellowed out a loud laugh.

"Prize chicken. Hence my hair." I pointed to my head. "This is where it gets crazy. Marla Maria has always wanted to open a pageant studio where she prepares girls for pageants from their hair to their walk. She could never do it when Chicken was alive, because Chicken used their money to enter Lady Cluckington into all sorts of chicken pageants."

"Don't forget to tell him that Marla Maria

wasn't the only one with dreams." Chicken stood in the middle of the floor with his thumb pointing to him. "I wanted to be on the cover of *Cock and Feathers* magazine. If Marla Maria didn't kill me, we'd probably be the owner of some dumb pageant studio."

"What? Is he here?" Jack Henry stood up. There was frustration in his voice. He ran his hands through his hair and then dropped them to his side. "I believe he was killed, but I just can't find solid evidence on who killed him, yet."

"Vernon is almost done with the autopsy. He will prove somehow that Marla Maria killed Chicken so she could get her hands on the money faster."

"Then the chicken should be dead too." He paced back and forth. "Did you see the agreement?"

"No, I haven't gotten that close. But I did get these tapes that Chicken told me to get." I pointed to the stack of VHS tapes I had left on the coffee table from earlier. "I'm getting closer to her because I agreed to be in the Orloff Beauty Pageant tomorrow in Lexington."

"You thought becoming blond and browbald was going to get you the title?" Jack Henry inched closer. His eyes narrowed as he took a better view of my nonexistent brows. His face grimaced. "When will the red puffiness go away?" He frowned in a sympathetic sort of way.

"I went to Girl's Best Friend to see if I could get in on some gossip, but all I got was Mary Anna doing to my hair what Marla Maria had told her to do." I sat back down.

"I don't want you to go. I want you to stop being a detective and leave the work to the forensics." His words were sudden, raw and angry. "I'm not saying Marla Maria is going to hurt you, but I'm saying you are aligning yourself with her. If she isn't the killer, someone who is happens to be watching her, putting you in danger. There is more to this murder than you know." He pointed directly at me. "When I agreed to listen to you because of your Betweener thingy, I didn't agree to put you in the middle. Besides, you have Zula to worry about."

"Oh! Now this is about Granny and you believing she attacked O'Dell Burns. Which, by the way, she did not!" I jabbed back at him. Suddenly I had confidence that I had never had. I brushed my hands through my hair. Was it the new blond hair giving me the strength? "I'm telling you, Marla Maria has motive and reason to have offed Chicken."

"Don't go to that pageant with her tomorrow," he warned. His dark eyes deepened to almost black. "I'm ordering you as the sheriff not to go."

Heat rose in my throat. "Fine. I'm going to bed." I agreed to his face, but my mind exploded with ideas on how I was going to solve Chicken's murder once and for all.

I stomped to the door and opened it.

"Good night." Jack Henry bent down to kiss me. I turned my head just in time for his lips to catch my cheek. "Fine. I'll call you tomorrow." He walked down the steps and turned back around. "Charge your phone."

Chapter 17

"Ugh." I rubbed my tired eyes when I looked in the mirror. Those tired eyes looked ghostly with blond hair. I used my fingertips to tap my cheeks, hoping to put a little color in them. Marla Maria would die if she saw me.

"You need coffee." Chicken stood behind me. "I've seen what Marla Maria does when her eyes look like that. And it ain't pretty."

Inwardly I groaned. I didn't want to find out what she did, nor did I want her to do it to me. After Jack Henry left last night, I had decided that I was going to pretend it was a "play dress-up" day, like I did when I was a little girl; get it over with and come home. There was no way I wanted to jeopardize my relationship with Jack Henry over a ghost and his might-be murder.

"Chicken." I walked into the kitchenette to make my first cup of much needed coffee. "I'm going to go to the pageant, but that is as far as I can go. This investigation is way over my head and Jack Henry said it's dangerous."

"Huh?" Chicken's face contorted in all directions. "You are doing great."

"Jack Henry said there is more to your murder than I know." I grabbed the creamer and poured some in my mug before I hit the BREW button on the Keurig.

Bang, bang, bang. "Emma Lee, open this door!" Charlotte beat on the interior door of my efficiency. The door that leads to the funeral home. "What in the hell happened to my office?"

Oh crap. I had totally forgotten about that little tidbit in the investigation. I had meant to tell Jack Henry about it and the missing keys, along with the golden feather I had found—Chicken had found—in Granny's kitchen, along with the dirt footprint.

I held my finger up to Chicken so he knew not to disappear on me because we still had to talk about the investigation and my role in the matter. He growled. Not happy.

"What the hell happened to you?" Charlotte's face scrunched up. Her nose curled. "Your freakin' hair is blond."

I ran my fingers through my hair. I kept forgetting about it, but everyone was so kind and happy to point it out.

"I'm going to be in a beauty pageant today," I said matter-of-factly.

"Geez." Charlotte had her cell phone in her hand. She started punching numbers on it. "I came here to find out what happened to my office. But now I've got to get you an appointment with Doc Clyde. I could kill Mom and Dad for leaving you in my care." She shook her head and turned back around. "Granny, you need to hop on that little moped of yours and tell your boyfriend that Emma Lee has a bad case of the Funeral Trauma." She paused and turned to face me again. "Are you seeing ghosts?"

"Hang up the phone." I glared at her.

"I don't know. She won't answer the question." Charlotte shifted her weight to one side. She held the phone up to her ear with one hand and looked at her manicure on her other hand. "What do you mean your moped was stolen? She mentioned you had lost your keys. OHMYGOD!" Charlotte yelled. "My office was torn up. Do you think they were trying to find something in there?"

"Here we go," I whispered, knowing Granny had to be giving Charlotte an earful.

"Yes. Call Jack Henry. I'll take care of Emma Lee, like always." She hit a button on her phone and slipped it back in her pocket. She smiled, softening her features. She put her arm around me. "Now, now." She patted me like I was some teenager who was going to explode on her. "I will call Mary Anna today and let her know what you did to your hair. I'm sure she will have a solution. Have you been taking your meds?" She took her phone out again and tapped the buttons.

"I don't need meds. Mary Anna is the one who did my hair." I put my hands on my hips. "And you have never taken care of me. Mom and Dad didn't leave *you* in charge."

"Oh grow up, Emma Lee." Charlotte flung her beautiful red hair that I was secretly jealous of and trotted back down the hall toward the offices, shaking her butt the entire way. "Jack Henry, can you send an officer over? Someone has broken into the funeral home."

I glanced over at the clock on my wall and quickly shut the door before I went back into the kitchenette to retrieve my coffee. If I knew Jack Henry, and I did, he wouldn't send anyone over but himself. He would make sure someone didn't break in and kill me. I was going to tell him all of that before he went all Robo-cop on me last night, but his behavior had made me forget.

"What were you saying to me?" Chicken wasn't happy with me. Hell, no one was happy with me. I might as well stick with the plan.

"I'm going to grab my stuff and head on over to Marla Maria's." I grabbed the charger on the counter to get my phone, but the end that was supposed to be hooked into the phone was dangling near the ground. "Crap."

I had forgotten to grab my phone out of the hearse.

"Come on." I grabbed my purse and keys. I had to get out of there before Jack Henry came. I wasn't in the mood to hear him yell at me again.

"My pleasure." Chicken rushed out behind me. We hopped into the hearse with Chicken taking his usual place with his arm draped around my shoulder. "Marla Maria is going to have a fit when she sees you."

And he was right. I tapped on the door of the double-wide and Marla Maria about had a woman-sized tantrum right there in front of me.

"Look at her!" Chicken was taking too much delight in the hissy fit Marla Maria was having. "She's shaking like a hound dog trying to shit a peach pit." He bent over in laughter.

"My reputation is on the line." She grabbed me. Her long nails dug into the fleshy part of my bicep. "Your hair is fabulous, but your brows are still red and those bags under your eyes are going to require surgery!"

"Surgery?" I shrugged away from her.

"Sit!" She ordered me to sit in the La-Z-Boy. She was all ready for the pageant in her leopard print leggings, tight black V-neck shirt, and black stilettos.

"That's my chair." Chicken protested.

"Really?" I questioned him out loud. "Now you question where I can sit?"

"What?" Marla Maria bit back.

"Nothing." I shook my head. I had to keep my mouth shut or Marla Maria would think I was crazy and not take me to the pageant.

"Good." Marla Maria turned and made her way into the kitchen. She opened the door of the refrigerator, her butt stuck up in the air as she rooted around. "There you are." She grabbed something and came back. "Close your eyes," she demanded and smacked something cold on my face.

"What is that?" I sniffed. "Is that bologna?" I would know the smell of Artie's Meat and Deli bologna in a minute. My Granny called it the best Kentucky round steak anywhere in the south.

"Don't you mind what it is." I heard her heels clicking away. I dared move. "I've got to get Lady Cluckington ready."

"Lady!" Chicken smacked his hands together. "This is a big pageant. She better look good, Marla Maria," Chicken warned as I lay there with my dignity stuck under a couple of pieces of meat. "Hurry, Emma Lee! Grab the other tape from the cabinet. You forgot one."

I peeled the edges of bologna back from my eyes and peeked at him.

"I did?" Quickly I jumped up and opened the cabinet. Lady Cluckington's squawking caught my attention. There was a tape in the far back, so I grabbed it and stuck it in my bag right before Marla Maria came through the door. One problem, the VHS was sticking out a little bit. *Please don't let her see it*, I repeated over and over in my brain.

I thrust the bologna in my mouth and threw my

body on the floor into the only yoga pose I could remember.

"What are you doing?" Displeasure was all over Marla Maria's face. "You can't eat bologna. It adds pounds and rolls to your figure. Spit it out!"

I opened my mouth and let the meat fall on the ground. Lady Cluckington flapped her wings, causing Marla Maria to drop her. She clucked her way over to the meat and gobbled it up.

"No! Lady!" Chicken scolded her. "You can't eat that."

It was too late. Lady had eaten it and was in the kitchen looking for more.

"This is not good." Chicken paced back and forth, running his hands through his black hair. Worry filled his eyes, deepening the lines in his crow's-feet.

"Oh good!" Marla Maria grabbed the VHS from my bag. "I'm so glad you brought your own music. Are you singing or doing a baton routine?"

My mouth dropped.

"You have to have a talent for the Ms. Orloff pageant," Chicken informed me.

Great. He had a habit of telling me things after the fact.

"Singing." I smiled.

"I've heard you sing and singing is not going

to give you the win," Chicken said and sat on the floor. Lady Cluckington hopped in his lap, though to the living, it looked like she was just hopping up and down.

"Great. Now let's get you ready." Marla Maria helped me off the floor and dragged me back to her lair of makeup.

Chapter 18

I could hardly enjoy the ride to Lexington because Marla Maria had made me shove the passenger seat in the Cadillac completely back and change bologna slices every few minutes.

"I'm going to stink." The smell was making my stomach curl.

Marla Maria drove with one hand, grabbed the bologna off my face with the other, flinging the meat to the backseat and at Lady Cluckington, who eagerly gobbled it up.

"Tell her to stop that." Chicken sat next to Lady in the backseat. I was nearly lying in his ghost lap. "She's going to get sick. Have you ever seen an Orloff get sick?"

Marla Maria was talented. She grabbed a couple

more pieces of bologna and slapped them across my eyes, covering the bridge of my nose. "Breathe in and out of your nose. This will help get oxygen to those gnarly bags."

I took a deep breath. *Cough, cough.* "I can't." I shot up in my seat, sending the bologna in the air, and it splattered on the windshield.

Bock, bock. Lady Cluckington went crazy in her cage, wings flapping, feathers flying.

"Stop." Chicken tried to soothe the hen, but she wasn't going to hear of it. "You are going to lose your feathers and you are the prettiest little Orloff entering the pageant." He made baby talk with the cranky fowl and clung to the cage. "Ouch!" Chicken let go of the cage wire and shook his hand in the air. "Did you just bite me? Bad Lady! Bad girl!"

"Just ignore her." Marla Maria had me turn back around. "Put that back on your face."

"I think I'm just going to rest my eyes, bare, and think about my song." *Please let me figure something out before I have to sing,* I said over and over in my head. I couldn't carry a tune and everyone in town knew it.

"Fine." Marla Maria reached back around and grabbed a tackle box. "Open it up and get out the number four foundation. We don't have a lot of time. Those bags took up a lot of time." She tapped the digital clock on the Cadillac dash. "We are going to make it just in time to register you."

I opened up the tackle box. There were all sorts of brushes, lipsticks, eyeliner pencils and many more things I didn't even recognize.

"I don't know what I'm looking for," I had to admit. "I don't wear a lot of makeup."

"Today you will be." Marla Maria reached over, and without missing a beat she grabbed a bottle of brown liquid with a red lid. "Shake it, open it, put some on your finger and then dab it on your face with the white sponge."

"White sponge." That was easy to find. I pulled the visor down and the mirror lit up and I followed Marla Maria's directions. I used the time to get some information. "So where are you going to open the pageant studio?" I knew she had told me before, but somehow I had to bring it up.

"My dearly departed Chicken has some land in Lexington that is not developed." She did the sign of the cross with her free hand. "Rest his unrested soul. Do you think he was murdered?"

"I . . ." My mouth dropped. A better question would be, *Do you think I killed my beloved Chicken?* "I don't know. I did hear you were going to have O'Dell Burns put him back."

It probably wasn't the right time to say something, but I never was good at timing.

"You know about that?" Marla Maria asked. "It was O'Dell Burns's idea."

Of course I knew about it. Marla Maria had forgotten she had already told me. A sure sign she wasn't able to keep her lies and facts straight. "What did you want the police to do? They had to dig up the coffin in order to let him have everlasting peace." I rubbed the makeup over my bags, which weren't nearly as dark as they had been.

"Dab. Dab!" Marla Maria grabbed the sponge and showed me what she meant while still being able to maneuver the back roads. "You don't think he is at peace?"

"I think that if he was murdered, he might be a little restless. Don't you?" I asked, wondering if she was going to start feeling guilty for killing him.

"He's dead." She shrugged. "It's not like he's haunting me or trying to contact me from the dead."

"Speak for yourself," I muttered while using the eyeliner on my eyelids.

"Use that same pencil to fill in your brows." She did a sweeping motion with her finger. She put both hands on the wheel and glanced over at me. "Do you think he really was killed? I just don't know when it would've happened. Why would someone want him dead?" she rambled on and on.

"What about the property? Would someone other than you want it?" I asked. Maybe she would give me a little insight to her motives to kill him, not that the money part wouldn't be enough.

"No." She shook her head. "It's nothing special. In the middle of nowhere in the woods. He promised me he would help me open up a pageant school and then he up and died on me."

"What about Lady?" Somehow, I had to get out the truth about the divorce papers and the agreement. "Did you always take good care of her?"

I knew the truth. Chicken knew the truth. Marla Maria knew the truth. Was she going to tell the truth was the real question.

"I'm not going to say it was easy sharing Chicken's heart with *her*." Marla Maria jerked her head to the backseat of the Cadillac. "How would you feel if that big hunk of a sheriff you have brought his gun to bed with y'all?" She looked over at me. Her mouth dropped. "You haven't slept with that hunk of man." That was quite a statement.

"I don't think that is any of your business." How did this questioning turn around on me? I hadn't seen this happen in the TV shows.

"You better do something to keep that man. He is fine and there are plenty of women who will give him what a man needs." She winked. "If you know what I mean."

"Jack Henry isn't like that." I crossed my arms in front of me. Suddenly she made me feel insecure. I patted my pocket for my phone. *Shit!* It was still on the passenger seat of the hearse. Dead. "He is caring and sincere. He loves me the way my hair was."

"He didn't try to kiss all over you when he saw your new hair color?" She asked and a fire burned on my insides. The more I thought about his lips searing down my neck, the more Marla Maria's words hurt.

"That is none of your business." I refused to look at her. I was pissed.

"Honey," her words were condescending, "if you think that little librarian look you have going is going to keep a man like Jack Henry Ross at home, you have another thing coming."

The more she yapped, the angrier I got and the more determined I was to see her behind bars.

"Here we are." Marla Maria pulled the Cadillac over to the entrance of the festival fairgrounds. She dug her hands down her shirt and propped her boobs up to high heaven, creating the deepest cleavage I had ever seen. My eyes about popped out of my head. "Oh honey, these are bought." She reached over and tapped my chest. "You could use some yourself," she quipped.

"Hi there," Marla Maria used her best Southern drawl and puckered her lips, giving the attendant an air kiss. "Is there a way I can pull up and let these beauties out?"

He bent down and looked in the back of the car at Lady Cluckington. His gaze slid to me and then directly to Marla Maria's breasts.

"Ma'am, the restricted parking is for patrons of the festival." The attendant had a hard time keeping his eyes off her chest.

"Tell the guy who you are." Chicken continued to calm a cranky Lady Cluckington.

"I'm Emma Lee Raines," I blurted out, trusting Chicken knew what he was talking about.

"Great." The guy didn't seem to be too impressed.

"Tell them who *I am*." Chicken patted his chest. "Tell them this is Lady Cluckington."

"We are here for Chicken Teater." I pointed to Lady. "That's Lady Cluckington."

"Hellfire." The man whipped off his festival hat and smacked it down on his legs. He bent down looking into the passenger window at Lady Cluckington. "I thought we had seen the last of you, beautiful girl." He dripped the biggest, brightest smile. The man looked at Marla Maria's boobs again. He darted his eyes back toward Lady. "We heard about Mr. Teater's body being dug up because they think someone killed him." He leaned into the car, eyes down on Marla Maria's boobs again, and whispered, "I bet that no-good wife of his did it." He dragged his finger across his neck and made a slicing noise. Marla Maria's nose flared. His lips kept smacking together. "The festival awaits the day she finds out about the monthly donations we still get from his estate. God rest his soul."

"Donations?" Marla Maria cried out.

"Thank you!" I shouted and gestured for Marla Maria to go.

Go she did. She didn't wait for the attendant to move. She stepped on the gas and there was no delay. I looked out the back window. The attendant threw his cap down and spit on the ground.

"That sonofabitch," Marla Maria screamed and continued to hit the steering wheel. "He gave everyone money but me!" She jabbed her fingernail at her chest.

She slammed on the brakes. I threw my hands

on the dashboard to keep me, my seat belt and all from being flung through the windshield.

"I swear . . ." She threw the gearshift to PARK and turned around. Chicken hugged Lady's cage and closed his eyes—tight. "You'd better kick the bucket soon, because I stuck around to get my fair share!"

Oh my! Did she just confess to the murder of Colonel Chicken Teater?

"If you stick to the agreement, you get your fair share!" Chicken screamed back at her. Too bad she couldn't hear him.

She jumped out of the Cadillac and slammed the door shut, causing me to jump. I unclipped my seat belt after I heard her tap on the trunk, signaling me to get out.

"Here goes nothing." I looked in the visor mirror one more time before flipping it up.

"Not one more word about Chicken," she scolded me like I was their child. "Do you hear me?" She opened the trunk using the key fob and grabbed a clothes hanger that was in a plastic bag. She whipped it in the air, causing the contents to fall to the ground while still holding the hanger. "Go put this on." She thrust it toward me.

"Oh no." I shook my head ferociously, catching

my reflection in the back window. The blonde was much blonder in the sunlight. "I'm not wearing that."

The sun also caught the plastic cover, exposing a pink dress. Not just a dress. A spaghetti strapped, laced-up-the-back, ballerina-style dress with all sorts of beads and bling on the bodice leading into a long puffy skirt made out of feathers. Chicken feathers.

"Yes you are." Marla Maria thrust the plastic at me again. "You are a student of mine that I'm taking on as pro bono. That is, until you get your five-thousand-dollar check today."

"Five thousand dollars?" I asked.

"Yes. You win today and you win five thousand dollars." She held the hanger up. I snatched the dress.

"I'll be right back." I darted in the direction of the cement block ladies' room.

Chapter 19

There was little to no room in the concrete-built bathroom. All the pageant contestants had to be in there at once, elbowing their way in front of the only mirror on the wall. And I use the word *mirror* loosely. It was more like those fun mirrors at the carnival that completely distort your body and face. But these girls didn't care. They were talented, using one hand to apply mascara while using the other to pin up their hair.

I dipped into the only open stall.

"No wonder," I muttered, regarding why the stall was free. The thin plywood door barely hung on to a hinge by one little crooked nail and urine and toilet paper filled the bowl to the rim. And the smell—I put my hand over my mouth so I wouldn't gag out loud. "Just get the dress on. Five thousand dollars."

"Excuse me"—I held the feather skirt up to my waist so it wouldn't drag on the dirty bathroom floor—"can you tie me up?" I asked a contestant who was not-so-patiently waiting in line for the wonky mirror.

"Suck in," she demanded. Her red dress had a feathered skirt too, only hers was maybe an inch past her butt cheeks. Her thin legs looked like chicken legs.

I turned around and looked at the jammed-in girls. I busted out in a fit of laughter. Everyone turned around and looked at me.

"I'm sorry," I busted out one more time. I pointed to several of the girls in front of me. "I'm sorry." I tried to apologize for my behavior. "We look like a bunch of chickens in a coop. Eek." My breath caught as the girl tugged the laces tighter.

"That will teach ya to call us chickens." The girl shoved me forward and out the bathroom door.

"You won't be getting the Miss Congeniality award," I shouted over my shoulder after hearing a fit of laughter coming from the gaggle of women, not to mention Chicken Teater was right outside the door, laughing. "Oh shut up," I grumbled. "I'm only doing this for you."

"They are just like a fussy henhouse in there."
He smacked his hand on his knee.

"Enough of the chicken jokes." I balled my fists
and stormed off to find Marla Maria. The quicker
I could get out of here, the better.

The fairgrounds had a few little kids' rides,
bringing back fond memories of how Mom, Dad
and Granny would take Charlotte and me to the
summer fairs to ride all the fun coasters until our
stomachs gurgled from the twirling and eating
super-sweet elephant ears.

Must get an elephant ear. My eyes followed my
nose to the staple of fair food—funnel cakes. Why
didn't they have one of these food trailers at the
Kentucky Cave Festival?

"I'll have . . ." I scanned the handwritten menu
taped to the glass window. "Oh my." My mouth
watered when I saw "deep-fried Twinkie."
"That!" I pointed to the sugary, artery-clogging
treat.

"You'd better not let Marla Maria see that."
Chicken's eyes lit up like a dark night sky full of
stars.

"Are you taking pleasure in this?" I asked. I
didn't care if Marla Maria saw me eat the deep-
fried goodness.

"What did you say?" The woman eyed me suspiciously with her hand out the window and my treat between her fingers.

"Nothing." I took the corndog-like dessert, grabbed a couple of napkins and stuffed the edges in the top of the dress. I didn't care if Marla Maria saw me eating it, but getting some on the dress was another issue.

Chicken and I walked to the arena where their owners were showing the chickens. Lady Cluckington wasn't until after the Ms. Orloff beauty pageant. I hoped that by then I would have some more answers.

"Why is it that everything tastes better on a stick?" I leaned my body a little forward, just in case of an oil drip, and took a big bite.

"Wait!" The scream came from the top of the bleachers near the announcer's booth. "Don't you dare put that in your mouth!" The sun peeked out of the fluffy white clouds, putting Marla Maria in the spotlight. She handed the announcer something before she screamed, "Drop it!" She climbed down the bleachers with her finger in the air. "I said drop it!"

"Uh-oh," Chicken warned. "I told you that you better be on the lookout for her."

Marla Maria's eyes stayed focused on mine. I

took another bite, a little more dramatically this time. Marla Maria was seething. Her hands and talon-like claws were stretched out in front of her. Her scrawny legs were trying to work double-time to get to me faster than a snake.

Everyone fell silent. Not even a cluck could be heard. All eyes watched as Marla Maria bolted over to me and snatched the Twinkie right out of my hands.

"What do you think you are doing?" Marla Maria glared at me while she flung the Twinkie into the air. "You can NOT get bloated before a pageant. This is what I will be teaching at my school—nutrition!"

She turned on her heels, picked up the Twinkie off the ground, and stomped over to a barrel made into a makeshift trash can.

The roar of a motorcycle, not to mention the flashing lights, announced the entrance of Sugar Wayne.

"Great. What is he doing here?" Marla Maria propped her fists on her waist, shifting her hips to the right.

"Yee-haw!" Chicken jumped around. "Now Lady Cluckington has a chance to win."

"Did you honestly think I wasn't going to find

you?" Sugar Wayne's hair was especially black today. Nothing was dripping—yet. "It's only the biggest day in Lady's career!"

"I can handle it, Sugar Wayne." Marla Maria grabbed me by the wrist and flung me around. "Come on. The pageant is almost ready to start, and you are contestant number one."

"I'm not going anywhere." Sugar walked behind us. Too close. "I'm going to finish what my best friend asked me to do, and you and that girl in the pink chicken costume won't stop me."

"Go away, Sugar!" Marla Maria squeezed my arm when I tried to turn around.

She practically dragged me. Sugar was on our heels.

"I was hoping you would forget after all of these years." Marla Maria jabbed back to Sugar.

"I haven't forgotten anything. Especially today." His twenty-seven-inch-long legs could barely keep up with us.

"That's right, Sugar. You keep at her!" Chicken ran along between Marla Maria and Sugar.

"What is so significant about today?" I stopped and jerked my arm away from Marla's claws.

"Do I know you?" Sugar panted and planted his hands on his knees trying to catch his breath. He tried to look at me and I tried not to look at him because the exercise he got from trying to keep up with Marla Maria had made him sweat. Which meant his hair was dripping.

"Nope." I shook the blond hair. Thankfully, it was a great disguise since I had no plans of telling Marla Maria how or why I knew Sugar Wayne.

"Today is the big day Chicken had been waiting for." Marla Maria dug her nails into Sugar's bicep, causing him to wince. "Four years and you aren't going to stop me."

"You are such a . . ." Sugar bit his lip. "Where is Lady Cluckington? I don't have time to worry with you. I have to get her ready."

Marla Maria put her hand out, spreading her fingers, her bright red fingernails jutting out like daggers. Her eyelashes lowered, creating a dark shadow on her cheek. Her voice was low, eerie: "You will not go near Lady Cluckington. She is my responsibility." Slowly she fisted her hand and leaving her pointer finger out she poked Sugar Wayne's chest. "Do you read me loud and clear?"

"Are you warning me?" Sugar puffed his chest out like a Banty rooster. Chicken stood between them with his mouth hanging open. "Are you trying to threaten me?" Sugar moved around in a circle. "I need a police officer." He turned to Marla Maria, whose finger was still pointed directly at

Sugar. He smacked it away. "Chicken might have been scared of you. But I am not. Did you kill my friend?"

Sugar stepped forward and came nose to breast with Marla Maria, only his eyes were pointing straight up to Marla Maria's eyes, not caring about her boobs, which was probably a first for him.

"Oh crap," Chicken warned. Marla Maria was visibly getting madder by the second. "I wish Sugar was the Betweener. He doesn't mess around."

I shot him a look that should have sent him back to the great beyond, or wherever he came from, or needed to get to. Unfortunately, the glare didn't work. He was still standing there, taking a lot of pleasure in his buddy standing up for him.

"Police officer!" Sugar Wayne shouted into the crowd of people who were walking by to get in the arena to see the pageant. Some had chickens, roosters, and other types of fowl on leashes. The damndest thing I had ever seen. "We have a murderer here!" He pointed to Marla Maria.

"I'm not going to stand here and be ruined by a low-life realtor who can't seem to stop his fake hair from dripping." Marla's sneer turned into an evil grin. There was a little too much pleasure in her face. "If you think I killed Chicken . . ." She stepped forward and bent down to get on his level. Through her perfectly gritted teeth, she said, "Prove it. Do you think a cop is going to believe you or me?" She straightened her shoulders. She grabbed me by the wrist. "Come on." She jerked me when she started to walk. "We don't have time for such lowlifes."

"I'll show you!" Sugar Wayne screamed, rolling up on his toes and screaming threats to Marla Maria through the crowd.

Marla Maria was firing mad. She blurted out all sorts of things about Sugar and how he had been a big problem in her marriage. She didn't know what Chicken had agreed to with Sugar because Chicken had agreed to do so many things with all sorts of people. God knows what he promised them. "That is why I'm getting this damn pageant over with and holding on to my property. I held up my end of the agreement." Marla Maria spouted.

"Agreement? What did your agreement say?" I asked.

She abruptly stopped, but I kept going. Her claws dug deeper into my skin as I chugged forward.

"Ouch!" I tried to jerk away. She wasn't letting go. She dragged me behind one of the food trail-

ers out of the way of everyone. "Let go of me." I
tried to jerk again.

"You listen to me, you little tart." Marla Maria
pulled me closer to her. Suddenly her beauty-
queen status was turning more into the evil queen.
"You heard me back there. I'm not sure what you
are up to, but I know damn good and well you are
snooping around—you and that hunk of a man of
yours. Oh"—she pointed a finger at me—"I tried
my hardest to come on to him, so you better watch
yourself."

With a hard jerk, I got my arm free. There were
marks where her nails had dug into my skin.

"As for Chicken," she shoved my shoulder causing me to lose my footing and fall onto the grassy
surface of the fairgrounds. "you let the dead rest.
Do I make myself clear?"

I nodded and jumped up. Fear knotted in my
stomach.

"I'm going to open my school with or without
anyone's help." She put her high-heeled shoe on
my thigh, leaving a dirt stain on my dress.

I gulped. It was the same dirt stain I had found
in Granny's kitchen.

"As a matter of fact, after we leave here, I'm
going to meet a contractor to build my studio
on Chicken's damn land. I don't give a shit who

knows about the agreement. I'm going through with my end of the deal." She put her hand out to help me up.

"I don't know what you are talking about." I helped myself up and pretended not to understand, for the safety of my life. "What agreement? Who knows what?"

"Don't play dumb with me." She glared. "Not even looking good will help me to like you more."

"Let me help you." I decided to play her game. "Maybe I can get the inside scoop from Jack Henry."

Her facial features slowly softened. She rubbed her chin.

"Welcome to the annual Ms. Orloff Beauty Pageant. Not only is the Ms. Orloff title very important today, but today is the long-awaited pageant for the amazing Orloffs themselves," the announcer blared over the intercom. "All of the Orloff hens that will be here have been going through extensive grooming, training and vigorous activities over the past five years just to be shown today." Applause echoed throughout the fairgrounds. "The winner will move on to the National Orloff Chicken Championship that is held every five years. Now, who is ready for some lovely women?"

Marla Maria darted her head around the food trailer to see what was going on.

"I might just take you up on that. But the one thing you need to know is that I didn't kill Chicken. I was going to divorce him because of that damn chicken and because he spent too much time with Sugar." She talked so fast it was hard to keep up. "He even tried to set Sugar and me up when I first met him. The nerve. Didn't that man know I adored him? After I told him I was leaving, he told me about the land he had bought and was going to build me a fancy beauty studio, but we had to get through with this last competition in four years. This is it."

I tried to follow her as closely as I could, but her words began to blur with the crowd screaming and the announcer going over the contest rules.

"He told me he had a trusted advisor with the particulars that would contact me after this event in the case something happened to him." She looked around the food stand again. "That stupid Sugar Wayne was helping him show Lady Cluckington and he has some sort of sick obsession seeing Chicken's dream come true."

"That's because he is a true friend." Chicken spat in the ground. He wasn't buying into her *I loved him so much* speech.

"Our first contestant is the lovely Emma Lee Raines, all the way from Sleepy Hollow, Kentucky." The announcer said my name over the intercom. "Come on out, Ms. Raines."

"Hurry! We are late!" Marla Maria shoved me out from behind the food trailer.

I ran like a chicken with my head cut off, darting in and out of the crowd in the pink dress. Pink feathers were flying.

Chapter 20

Once I was onstage, the announcer started reading off my stats, like my height, weight, talent and occupation. Things I didn't have a clue how he knew. I didn't care. I was here to do my job as a Betweener and get Chicken to the other side.

My mind was boggled with all the information Marla Maria had spit at me right before I took the stage. The pageant lights hung down from the open metal building, shining directly on me. It was hard to see out into the crowd. But I could make out Chicken and Marla Maria, who must have gone back and gotten Lady Cluckington out of her cage, because Lady was neatly tucked in Marla's lap.

Chicken paid no attention to me as I walked

down the runway, showing off my ballet chicken-feathered dress, doing my best princess wave. Marla Maria kept putting her hands up to her face and pointing to her lips as she mouthed *smile*.

"The lovely Ms. Emma Lee Raines is going to be singing for us tonight." The announcer pointed to the guy in the audio/visual booth.

"I . . ." A small childlike voice came out of me. I had made no preparation to sing. As a matter of fact, Marla Maria and I had only discussed it earlier and then I didn't think she was serious.

Like slow motion, I watched the audiovisual guy take the VHS and put it in the old VHS tape player.

"Stop!" I screamed and put my hand out when I realized it was Chicken's home footage tape I had taken earlier from Marla Maria's cabinet. She must have thought it was my talent tape when she saw it in my bag.

It was too late. The video played a scene from the life of Marla Maria and Chicken Teater's home life.

"What the hell?" Marla Maria held tight to Lady Cluckington when she stood up. "Stop that tape right this instant!" Marla Maria stomped her heeled feet.

The video guy kept pushing buttons, but the

video wouldn't stop. He said something about it being old. But Marla Maria wasn't going to have any part of it. She stomped over to the audiovisual booth. She held Lady tight to her chest with one hand while she pushed buttons with the other.

In the meantime, Chicken was arguing with Marla Maria on the tape about the beauty pageant. Marla Maria was in perfect position for the camera angle when she shouted at Chicken, "That pageant is stupid. Raising Orloff hens is stupid. If you want to hang around stupid and ignorant people all of your life, fine with me! I want a divorce!"

The crowd fell silent. Marla Maria jerked the old VHS player causing the wiring to pull out of the electrical socket. Sparks flew everywhere.

The microphone stand was in front of me and the crowd stared at me.

"Old McDonald had a farm," I sang out, "E-I-E-I-O. And on his farm he had a chicken. E-I-E-I-O." I gestured for the crowd to sing along. "With a . . ." I put my hand up to my ear. Reluctantly the crowd sang *cluck, cluck here and a cluck, cluck there.*

The videotape machine must've been on the same circuit as one of the spotlights, because one of the two lights were out, allowing me to see Marla Maria being dragged out from underneath the metal building. At first I thought it might have been one of the Orloff pageant committee members dragging her out, but it wasn't. It was Sugar Wayne. He had Marla Maria in one hand and Lady in the other.

I jumped off the stage, running as fast as I could to see what he was doing. But I lost them in the crowd. I made it to the parking lot to see if they were there. There was a cloud of dust leaving the parking lot and turning left onto the main road. It was Chicken's red Cadillac.

Chapter 21

"Wait!" I screamed, running after Marla Maria with my arms flapping above my head. "Wait for me!"

I flipped off the stupid heels, which I should have probably done hours ago, and patted around for my cell phone while continuing to run on the hard gravel road.

"Ouch, ouch, ouch." My feet stung under me. "Damn." I stopped when I got to the road and realized I was still in the stupid dress with no pockets, and no cell phone. Not that my cell was charged up anyway.

"Hop in." The old beat-up Chevy pulled over and the driver rolled down the window. "If you want to follow her, I said to hop in."

"What the hell is that low-life no-good sonofa-bitch doing in my truck?" Chicken Teater stood in front of his old Chevy with his arms out as if the driver could see him.

"You . . ." I swallowed hard. "You are Marla Maria's neighbor."

"I'm not wasting time." He gestured for me to come on. "I'm out of here if you aren't going with me."

Oh . . . I hesitated. These were the scenes—the scary scenes—that made up the TV crime shows. But I was stuck. I was sure Marla Maria had been banned from the pageant after what she had said on the tape. I didn't trust a fairground full of chicken lovers when they only associated me with Marla.

"Oh . . ." I darted back and forth between the truck and the parking lot trying to decide whether or not to get in the truck with a stranger—much less him. The truck started moving forward. "Wait!"

John Deere hat guy jerked forward when he slammed on the brakes. Chicken stood his ground, still standing in front of the truck. He didn't take his eyes off John Deere guy.

"I'm coming." I ran around the truck and shrugged my shoulders when I passed Chicken.

"You are a traitor!" Chicken didn't move. "I don't know what kind of Betweener you are, but I won't be passing your name along to anyone else!"

I hopped in the old truck and reached for a seat belt.

"Truck is too old for a seat belt." John Deere pushed the pedal and lurched the old Chevy forward, right through Chicken Teater's ghost.

"Eek!" I shrieked when I saw the truck hit Chicken and I shut my eyes, squeezing them tight.

"I won't let this sonofabitch steal my wife or my truck! Or my Betweener!" I heard Chicken squeal.

I barely opened my eyes and I was relieved to see Chicken was facedown with his arms outstretched on the hood of the truck.

"Duckie Finney." Duckie held his hand out for me to shake.

"Emma Lee Raines." I took his hand. What was it with Marla Maria and men with fowl names?

Suddenly he wasn't as scary as I had thought he was when I watched him from behind the tree when Chicken's coffin was being dug up. "Why were you watching Chicken being dug up? And why are you always over at Marla Maria's?"

There was no reason *not* to ask blunt questions. I was already in the car and if he was going to kill me, I might as well go down with answers that would satisfy my curiosity.

"I. Love. Her." Tears dripped out of Duckie's eyes. "She and Chicken had a volatile relationship. There was no doubt in my mind they loved each other, but I can give her all the attention she needs."

"Duckie, where are we going?" The Chevy was going in the opposite direction of Sleepy Hollow, toward Lexington.

"I told Marla Maria I would meet her at the property to give her ideas for the beauty school." He used the sleeve of his shirt to wipe the snot off his nose, grossing me out. "I'm going to build it for her for free." He looked over at me. "I love her."

"I understand you love her." I smiled. My throat tightened.

"That sonofabitch killed me to get my woman!" Chicken shouted from the hood of the truck.

That's exactly what I was thinking.

"I saw you snooping around her house when she was with Lady." His hands gripped the steering wheel, causing his knuckles to whiten. I couldn't help but picture them around my neck.

Nervously, I plucked the feathers from the skirt of my dress.

"I need to get you out of here." Chicken's eyes deepened. He looked determined to do something. "Don't let him get near my ladies." It warmed my heart to hear Chicken refer to Marla and Lady as his ladies, but my gut was anything but warm. It was stone cold as I feared for my life.

"I watch over Marla Maria." Duckie looked back at the road. I noticed the truck was speeding up. I gripped the handle on the door, wondering if I opened it and jumped out if I might make it. "What were you looking for?"

"Nothing," I lied. "I wanted to be her first student at the school."

"I was thinking about going to Eternal Slumber and making some pre-need funeral arrangements, but I don't do business with liars." Duckie's Southern drawl was so deep I had to focus on listening to understand what he was saying to me. "You, Emma Lee Raines, are a liar. I dug into your past. You have never been able to hold a candle to your sister, Charlotte. Though I do think you are a pretty girl."

"Why does everyone say that?" I was annoyed and fed up. "I'm tired of everyone comparing me to her. We are two different people."

"Your hair looks great. Marla Maria told me she was having you go blond for the pageant, but it looks like you screwed up her chances of getting the property that is rightfully hers." Duckie's eyes narrowed. "Which means my woman won't be happy and will have to be stuck in the double-wide the rest of her life." He shook his head. "Such a shame too. She really wants to share her beauty with the world. Chicken Teater held her back from shining, you know."

"I know Chicken loved her." I wasn't going to let him talk bad about Chicken. "Duckie, did you kill Chicken to get Marla Maria's heart?"

He slammed on the brakes, making the Chevy come to a screeching halt. Chicken flew off the truck and onto the street before he appeared between Duckie and me in the cab of the truck, in his usual position, only the other arm was planted around my shoulders.

"You think I would make her heart hurt? I'm trying to help her get over Chicken." Duckie took off his John Deere cap and revealed the most beautiful head of blond hair. The curls clung tight to his head from the sweat the cap had created. "I would never hurt her. That included killing her husband. Not that I didn't want to get my hands on him when Marla Maria had cooked him a roast dinner one night and he spent the night at the Watering Hole with that no-good realtor friend of his."

"Sugar Wayne?" I asked, and oddly, believed that Duckie wouldn't hurt a fly.

"Yeah, that's his name. Which reminds me"—he pushed the pedal to the metal—"I know he is in love with my Marla Maria. Chicken was loyal to the wrong people in his life and now Marla Maria is paying for it."

"Slow down." I held on for dear life as Duckie used the truck as the fastest roller coaster in the world. The curves and winding road made my stomach do somersaults. "Why are we in such a hurry?"

"Didn't you see him throw Marla Maria and Lady Cluckington into the Cadillac?"

"Sugar?" I asked.

"The police need to be looking at Sugar Wayne." He got my attention.

"Go on." I was curious as to why he thought that.

"I told you I'm in love with Marla Maria. I checked out everyone in her life like I did you." He pointed at me as we turned on a dirt road. "He claims he was Chicken's friend."

"He is my friend, you shmuck!" Hatred dripped from Chicken's lips.

"His real-estate business is dying. It's been dying. He sold Chicken this property years ago, knowing it was going to be worth millions when they put in the new interstate between here and Ohio." He eased the truck between some overgrown brush. "He wanted to be an Orloff chicken dealer like Chicken and Marla Maria, only he wasn't able to afford it. So he got knee-deep into cockfighting using those gold-and-black cocks."

"He's lying!" Chicken tried to punch him again like he had back at the trailer park, but it didn't bother Duckie like before.

"Gold and black?" I questioned, remembering the feather from Granny's kitchen. The shoeprint still came from Marla Maria—it had to.

"Yes. He is using the gold-and-black cocks to cockfight and gamble, all on the back part of Chicken's property."

My jaw dropped.

"When Marla Maria took me to see the property a few weeks ago, we saw the remains of the fighting. So I started to follow Sugar Wayne around. I even hid in the bushes while he was hosting a fight." Duckie held his finger up to his mouth. "Shh. They are here."

"Here where?" I looked around at the wooded area.

"This is Chicken's property. It's worth half a million."

"Why would Marla Maria want to build a school here?" I questioned. Some things didn't add up. Especially the cockfighting theory. "And you saw the fighting going on?"

"I told you there is an interstate coming through here, which will give Marla more money. It won't take up all the property. But it will give Marla Maria visibility from the interstate and she can open up a strip mall for others to join her. Making her more money and more business."

"So why would Sugar kill me?" Chicken asked a great question.

"None of this makes Sugar a killer," I said. "Marla Maria could have had the motive to kill him with the property in some sort of hold until she held up her agreement."

"I'm telling you. The police need to be looking at Sugar Wayne and not my Marla Maria." He opened his door. "You slide out on my side. I don't want to alarm them we are here in case I need to save my girls."

"They are *my* girls!" Chicken stood next to him with his fists raised, ready to fight.

I did what Duckie told me to do. I wasn't convinced of anything. All I wanted was to go home to my dead clients, put on their good-bye parties and eat at Bella Vino with Jack Henry. Maybe even have a glass of sweet tea with Granny while sitting in one of the rocking chairs at the Sleepy Hollow Inn.

Duckie grabbed the tire wrench out of the back of Chicken's truck. I followed him through the brush breaking all sorts of old branches.

"Please be careful where you are stepping." He looked down at my bare feet. "Where are your shoes?"

"Marla had me in heels and they hurt. I kicked them off."

Duckie let out a heavy sigh. He leaned his body up against a tree, untied both of his shoes and handed them to me. "Here. I can't let a lady go barefoot through the woods." He held one of his feet up in the air showing me his sock foot. "I've got socks I can wear."

"Thanks." I smiled and took his shoes. I had to put the grossness of inserting my bare feet into someone else's shoes out of my mind. "Now what do we do?"

"I think he has kidnapped Marla Maria and is going to sell Lady Cluckington." His eyes looked hollow. "Or worse . . ." he paused, " . . . use Lady Cluckington as a fighter."

"A fighter?" I asked. This entire situation was going way beyond my sleuthing expertise. I was just a funeral girl from Sleepy Hollow, not Kate Beckett from *Castle*. The ghosts were supposed to tell me what happened to them, not put me in the middle of it.

"Sugar Wayne would never do that to Lady Cluckington." Chicken wasn't buying anything Duckie was selling me.

"Hear him out." I was so tired of Chicken defending Sugar Wayne.

"Hear who out?" Duckie stopped. He turned around and looked me up and down before he put his hand on my forehead.

I jumped back.

"What are you doing? Get your hands off me." I turned to run back but he grabbed me. This was it. Duckie was the killer. I just knew it. All the stuff he said about Sugar was believable. Too believable. I freed my arm and ran as fast as I could while darting in and out of the brush until I got to a clearing.

I stopped when I saw Sugar, Marla Maria and Lady Cluckington, standing with a slew of other people.

"Wait!" Duckie squawked and stood next to me. He was bent over trying to catch his breath. "I was just making sure you weren't talking to someone else. I read you got the Funeral Trauma."

"Shh." I nodded toward the group of people. "Besides," I whispered, "I never had anything called the Funeral Trauma."

I glared at Chicken. I wished he could read my mind, because I was giving him a piece of it for making me talk to him out loud.

"Move it." The gruff voice came from behind me. A hard round something dug into the small of my back. "I said walk."

I'd seen enough TV shows to know to throw my hands up in the air and walk. We did what we were told.

"That dirty, no good sonofabitch." Chicken knew exactly who was behind us. "It's that dirty bartender from the Watering Hole."

"*Thank you*," I mouthed to Chicken. I was glad he was there to be my eyes for me.

"Look what I found lurking in the woods." The bartender had us walk straight over to the crowd that stood circled around a scared Lady Cluckington and big old cock in a chicken pen, ready to be let out to kill Lady; he was big enough to win a fight.

"Are you here to watch me train *my* prize chicken?" Sugar's gritty smile was smarmy and scary. "Did you think I didn't recognize you, funeral girl?"

"You can't possibly use Lady Cluckington to help train a cock to fight." I gestured toward her. "She's a helpless princess. What will it teach your bird?"

"You aren't so stupid, are you? He will kill her, taste her blood, and want more." He raised his voice. "He will bring me millions, especially with my fighting ring going on right here."

"Where are your shoes?" Marla Maria asked.

"This is going on and all you can ask me is where my shoes are?" I couldn't believe her.

"Beg him not to use Lady!" Chicken was desperate. "Tell him I won't hold up my end of the deal."

"If you use Lady, you won't be holding up your end of the deal," I blurted out.

"He's dead, thanks to me." He laughed.

"What?" Marla Maria darted toward him with her claws in the air going straight for his eyes. The bartender aimed at her over my shoulder and clicked the trigger, sending Marla Maria to the ground. Another shot rang out and he fell forward into me, sending me to the ground and landing on top of me.

"Get up! Get up!" I screamed, trying to push him off me. I looked at my hand and there was blood all over it. The chickens were going crazy with fear.

Sugar bent down next to me. I noticed in the dirt that his footprint was the same footprint I had found in Granny's kitchen, not to mention the feathers on the cock were exactly the same as the feather I had found there too.

"Don't you move!" Jack Henry shouted. I couldn't see him because the big burly guy was on top of me, but I could hear him and his heavy footsteps along with other footsteps.

"Stand up and slowly back away," Jack Henry ordered. Sugar did what Jack Henry told him to do.

Chapter 22

"Go over it again." Chicken asked me to ask Jack Henry one more time how Sugar Wayne had killed him.

The lights in the Sleepy Hollow Police Station interrogation room flickered as we sat there waiting for Marla Maria to hobble in to hear how Sugar Wayne was involved. The bartender's shot had grazed her in the knee. "Be careful. I have to strut my stuff on the pageant runway when I get my school built, so save my knee!" She had screamed the entire time she was being put into the ambulance. Chicken had me grab Lady to get her as far away from the crime scene as possible, only Jack Henry had other plans for me.

He was not happy to have found me there after

he shot the bartender and pulled me from underneath him. He then hauled me off to the station to interrogate me to find out what I knew.

After telling him all the clues I had found, he told me how they all fit together.

"Tell him to listen carefully." He referred to Chicken Teater before he opened the door and helped Marla Maria to a chair next to me. "I knew something was fishy when Emma Lee told me Chicken had a secret video camera with which he was taping his house to make sure no one was tampering with Lady Cluckington." Jack Henry swallowed hard. He knew what was about to come.

"You mean to tell me . . ." Marla Maria was starting to get angry at Chicken all over again.

"Let me finish." Jack Henry put his hands out to shush her. "I sent my officers back to the double-wide. I knew you weren't home because Emma Lee told me you were going to the Lexington fairgrounds"—he pointed at me—"which I told you not to do. You obviously didn't listen." He reached over and plucked a feather from my dress.

He blew it in the air. We sat there in silence as he continued to tell how he figured out Sugar Wayne had killed Chicken.

"Emma kept telling me about some agreement."

"Oh that!" Marla Maria's hand plunged down her shirt and pulled out a napkin. She flattened it out on the interrogation table. For a second, I thought she was using a napkin to blot her boob sweat. "Here it is."

My mouth dropped. "An agreement on a napkin? Are you kidding me?" I glared at Chicken.

"What? We did make the agreement while we were pretty loaded at the Watering Hole."

"Who are you talking to?" Marla Maria asked.

"She has the Funeral Trauma." Jack Henry came to my defense. "Anyway, my guys found the secret recorder and there was a tape in there. Chicken's last tape. It clearly showed Marla Maria pouring Chicken some sweet tea and handing him a glass. That was when Sugar came to visit and made his agreement with him about taking care of Lady if something happened to him. Chicken got up . . ."

Jack Henry and Chicken were talking at the same time.

"I got up and walked over to see if Marla Maria was out of earshot," Chicken recalled.

"When Chicken got up, you can clearly see Sugar Wayne put something in the tea pitcher and refilling Chicken's glass. He was going to kill Marla Maria too, but then . . ."

"I told him he could date and marry Marla Maria if I was dead so he could keep an eye on Lady since I knew he had always had a little thing for Marla," Chicken said.

"That is when you see Chicken gulp down the glass of tea, and Sugar refilling it yet again. When Marla Maria comes in to pour herself some more tea, Sugar accidentally knocks over the poisoned pitcher of tea, because he was seriously considering the fact he might get to marry you." Jack Henry pointed to Marla Maria.

"We looked into Sugar Wayne and that is when we connected how he sold the property to Chicken. When we went to check out the property, we found remains of the cockfighting going on there and put a couple of undercover guys on him. That's how we knew he was going to do something to Marla Maria and Lady, because Marla Maria wouldn't date him and the agreement was going to be completed after Lady's big competition today." Jack Henry ran his hands through his hair. Even in the dark interrogation room, he looked hot and hunky, making me want to jump up and kiss him, but I refrained when he continued. "We also went to Sugar's real-estate office." Jack Henry took out a document and pushed it in front of me. "Chicken and Sugar had a signed document from a lawyer and a witness. The witness was the bartender from the Watering Hole."

Jack Henry had shot the bartender in the back of the thigh, making him fall on me and pass out. Currently, he was undergoing surgery at the hospital to remove the bullet before they shipped him off to prison alongside Sugar Wayne.

"But it clearly states that if you"—he nodded toward Marla Maria—"didn't hold up your end of the deal, he got the land. Your end of the deal was the competition."

"But Lady didn't compete because he grabbed both of us from the beauty pageant." Marla Maria looked over at me and said, "By the way, you won't be my first student. You clearly aren't beauty-queen material."

"Good! I only did it for the investigation anyway," I blurted out and then covered my mouth.

"You are a cop now?" She crossed her hands over her chest and cocked one of her penciled-on eyebrows high.

"No, but I didn't want you to get your claws into him." I pointed to Jack Henry.

"Ladies, can we please get through this. I'm tired and I have a table waiting at Bella Vino." He looked at me and winked. Immediately, I straightened in my chair and zipped my lip.

"Luckily, the lawyer on the signature was at the cockfight so I'm pretty sure we can get him disbarred and you will get the property regardless." Jack Henry delivered the news like Marla Maria had won the competition anyway.

"That's wonderful news!" Marla Maria clasped her hands together. "I can get Duckie to start right away."

"O'Dell Burns was at the wrong place at the wrong time." Jack Henry reminded me about O'Dell's attack and I recalled seeing Sugar Wayne that very night, right before I had gone to Granny's. "Sugar Wayne heard you arguing with him. He knew you were snooping about Chicken and how you had gone to the Watering Hole. You were in his way. Everyone was around to hear you threaten O'Dell, and he used it against you and attacked O'Dell, making you look like a suspect."

Everything he was telling me made my head swirl. I had to take several deep breaths.

"Duckie isn't involved anyway?" I asked.

"No. He is just a good neighbor looking out for

Marla Maria." Jack Henry shut the file. "I got the lab results from Vernon Baxter. Chicken's tea was laced with arsenic. Large doses.

Chicken stood behind Jack Henry shaking his head.

"Please tell my Marla Maria I'm sorry I thought she killed me." Chicken appeared next to Marla and tried to stroke her hair.

She must have felt him because she looked up with tears in her eyes.

"No matter what you think, I loved Chicken. I really did." A tear dropped. I reached over, took a Kleenex from the tissue box and handed it to her. "I was tired of being the second love of his life. But I couldn't be without him."

Lady clucked happily in the cage by the door. The cock was next to her in his cage. He was just a baby. Never fought a day in his life. Marla Maria wanted to keep him too. She must have loved Chicken because she was willing to care for them both.

My bag from the pageant was also on the floor. I had no idea how Jack Henry had gotten it but I assumed one of the undercover officers who was trailing Sugar Wayne had picked it up.

"I'm sure he loved you too." I stroked her arm to give her some comfort.

"I'm going to take you ladies back to Marla Maria's so you can get on with your lives and Emma Lee can grab her hearse." Jack Henry helped us out of the station to his cruiser. I got to sit up front.

None of us said anything the entire way back to the trailer park. Marla Maria was exhausted, so she grabbed both cages and got out of the cruiser.

"I'll pick you up after you change?" Jack Henry plucked another feather. He reached through Chicken, who was sitting right next to me, and tickled my nose with it.

"I'll be ready." I looked around Chicken to see him. "I'm starving."

I got out of the car, retrieved my bag from the trunk and waved him off.

"Well, let's go." I exhaled, thinking I should say something profound to Chicken. I got in the hearse and started it up. "Let's go," I said again, ready for Chicken to sit next to me with his arm draped around my shoulder.

I waited a couple of minutes. Nothing. I glanced over at the empty spot where I had gotten used to seeing Colonel Chicken Teater. My heart sank. He was gone. He had crossed over.

Chapter 23

nhale. Exhale." Hettie Bell raised her hands over her head and lowered them.

Granny, Mable Claire and Beulah Paige all did what Hettie Bell told them to do.

"Look at all y'all this early in the morning." I had stopped for a big cup of coffee from Higher Grounds and decided to go see how Granny had taken the news about O'Dell Burns.

"You should be doing this too. I'm sure your stress level is out of this world." Hettie Bell stood up and put her hands on her hips before she went over to help Mable Claire into some position.

"I'm fine," I assured her.

Mable Claire jingled her way around until she

fell on her butt. Change scattered all over the front porch. She rushed around picking it up.

"You should probably clean out your pockets before you come to yoga." Granny bent down and picked up some items for her. "My key!" Granny held up the small moped key she had left in Charlotte's office. Her eyelids lowered. The wrath of Granny was upon Mable Claire. "Did you steal my moped?"

Mable Claire fumbled around, twirling her fingers. "I . . . I . . ." She took a deep breath and put her shoulders back before dropping her hands to her sides. "Yes I did. You are going to kill someone on that thing."

"Granny, calm down," I tried to talk some sense into Granny, though I knew she didn't hear a word of it. "Maybe she did it to save you from doing harm to yourself or worse . . . others."

"Yes." Mable Claire took a few steps backward as Granny took a few steps toward her. "Exactly what Emma Lee said. You are my dearest friend and I want to keep it that way."

Before Granny did any harm to poor Mable Claire, she inhaled deeply and said, "I have customers to cook breakfast for." She turned to Hettie Bell. "This is not a yoga studio. I suggest you get that building open and start doing your classes there."

Granny was the true Southern woman. She held her red head high and marched into the Inn. But not before turning around to get in the last word.

"Emma Lee, I need you to go retrieve my moped." She disappeared inside the Inn.

"It's behind Artie's Deli and Meats," Mable Claire whispered, looking a little guilty. "Behind the Dumpster. If you hurry I'm sure you can make it before the trash service gets there today."

"Thanks," I said before I darted down the stairs and across the square, which was filled with visitors coming for the last day of the Kentucky Cave Festival.

Artie's had a big handwritten sign in the window about free doughnuts. Who was I to give up a free doughnut? The moped could wait a few more minutes.

I stood in the cashier line, where they were handing out the delicious pastry. The magazine rep was restocking the magazine section in the front. I snickered when I saw *Cock and Feathers* but stopped when I saw the headline and picture.

Special Edition: Chicken Teater (owner of Lady Cluckington) is more famous in death than in life.

There was a split picture on the cover. One was of me onstage in the terrible dress, singing "Old McDonald," and the other was of Marla Maria ripping out the VHS tape player. There was a small circular photo of Chicken Teater strategically placed between the two photos.

"OhmyGod." I picked up the magazine and reread the headlines. I laughed. "I guess he made it onto the cover of *Cock and Feathers* after all."

"Hey." The husky voice behind me chuckled. "That's the guy that sent me to you." A chubby, hairy finger reached over my shoulder and pointed to Chicken's picture. "He said you can help me."

Read on for a sneak peek at the next

Ghostly Southern Mystery!

A
GHOSTLY
DEMISE

Available Fall 2015 from Witness!

Find out where it all began!

A
GHOSTLY
UNDERTAKING

is available now!

C ephus Hardy?"
    Stunned. My jaw dropped when I saw Cephus Hardy walk up to me in the magazine aisle of Artie's Meat and Deli admiring the cover of *Cock and Feathers*, where my last client at Eternal Slumber Funeral Home, Chicken Teater, graced the cover with his prize Orloff Hen, Lady Cluck-ington.

"I declare." A Mac truck could've hit me and I wouldn't have felt it. I grinned from ear to ear.

Cephus Hardy looked the exact same as he did five years ago. Well, from what I could remember from his social visits with my momma and daddy and the few times I had seen him around our small town of Sleepy Hollow, Kentucky.

His tight, light brown curls resembled a baseball helmet. When I was younger, it amazed me how thick and dense his hair was. He always wore polyester taupe pants with the perfectly straight crease down the front, along with a brown belt. The hem of his pants ended right above the shoelaces in his white patent leather shoes. He tucked in his short-sleeved plaid shirt, making it so taut you could see his belly button.

"Momma and Daddy live in Florida now, but they are going to be so happy when I tell them you are back in town. Everyone has been so worried about you." I smiled and took in his sharp pointy nose and rosy red cheeks. I didn't take my eyes off him as I put the copy of *Cock and Feathers* back in the rack. I leaned on my cart full of groceries and noticed he hadn't even aged a bit. No wrinkles. Nothing. "Where the hell have you been?"

He shrugged. He rubbed the back of his neck.

"Who cares?" I really couldn't believe it. Mary Anna was going to be so happy since he had just up and left five years ago, telling no one—nor had he contacted anyone since. "You won't believe what Granny is doing."

I pointed over his shoulder at the election poster taped up on the front of Artie's Meat and Deli's storefront window.

"Granny is running against O'Dell Burns for mayor." I cackled, looking in the distance at the poster of Zula Fae Raines Payne all laid back in the rocking chair on the front porch of the Sleepy Hollow Inn with a glass of her famous iced tea in her hand.

It took us ten times to get a picture she said was good enough and agreed to use it on all her promotional items for the campaign. Since she was all of five foot four, her feet dangled and she didn't want people to vote on her size, therefore, the photo was from the lap up. I told Granny that I didn't know whom she thought she was fooling. Everyone who was eligible to vote knew her and how tall she was. She insisted. I didn't argue anymore. No one, and I mean no one, wins an argument against Zula Fae Raines Payne. Including me.

"She looks good." Cephus raised his brows, lips turned down.

"She sure does." I noted.

For a seventy-seven-year-old and twice widow, Granny acted like she was in her fifties. I wasn't sure if her red hair was still hers or if Mary Anna kept it up on the down-low, but Granny would never be seen going to Girl's Best Friend unless there was some sort of gossip that needed to be heard. Otherwise, she wanted everyone to see her as the good Southern belle she was.

"Against O'Dell Burns?" Cephus asked. Slowly he nodded in approval.

It was no secret that Granny and O'Dell had butted heads a time or two. The outcome of the election was going to be interesting to say the least.

"Yep. She retired three years ago, leaving me and Charlotte Rae in charge of Eternal Slumber."

It was true. I was the undertaker of Eternal Slumber Funeral Home. It might make some folks skin crawl to think about being around dead people all the time, but it was job security at its finest. O'Dell Burns owned Burns Funeral, the other funeral home in Sleepy Hollow, which made him and Granny enemies from the get-go.

O'Dell didn't bother me though. Granny didn't see it that way. We needed a new mayor and O'Dell stepped up to the plate at the council meeting, but Granny wouldn't hear of it. So the competition didn't stop with dead people; now Granny wants all the living people too. As mayor.

"Long story short," I rambled on and on, "Granny married Earl Way Payne. He died and left Granny the Sleepy Hollow Inn. I don't know what she is thinking running for mayor because she's so busy taking care of all of the tourists at the Inn. Which reminds me." I planted my hands on my hips. "You never answered my question. Have you seen Mary Anna yet?"

"Not yet." His lips curved in a smile." I came to see you first. Cephus Hardy sent me."

"She's done real good for herself. She opened Girl's Best Friend Spa and has all the business since she's the only one in town. And—" I wiggled my brows, rambling on without letting him get a word in. "She is working for me at Eternal Slumber."

A shiver crawled up my spine and I did a little shimmy shake thinking about her fixing the corpses' hair and makeup. Somebody had to do it and Mary Anna didn't seem to mind a bit.

I ran my hand down my brown hair that Mary Anna had recently dyed since my little stint as a blond. I couldn't do my own hair, much less someone else's. Same for the makeup department.

I never spent much time in front of the mirror. I worked with the dead and they weren't judging me.

"Emma Lee?" Doc Clyde stood at the end of the magazine aisle with a small shopping basket in the crook of his arm. His lips set in a tight line. "Are you feeling all right?"

"Better than ever," my voice escalated when I pointed to Cephus. "Especially now that Cephus is back in town."

"Have you been taking your meds for the Funeral Trauma?" He ran his free hand in his thin hair, placing the few remaining strands to the side. His chin was pointy and jutted out even more as he shuffled his thick-soled doctor shoes down the old tiled floor. "You know it's only been nine months since your accident. And it could take years for the symptoms to go away."

"Funeral Trauma," I muttered and rolled my eyes.

Cephus just grinned.

The Funeral Trauma.

A few months back I had a perilous incident with a plastic Santa Claus right here at Artie's Meat and Deli. I had walked down from the funeral home to grab some lunch. Artie thought it was a good idea to put a life-sized plastic Santa on the roof. It was a good idea until the snow started melting and the damn thing slid right off the roof just as I was walking by, knocking me square out. Flat.

I woke up in the hospital seeing ghosts of the corpses I had buried six feet deep. I thought I had gone to the great beyond. But I could see my family and all the living.

I told Doc Clyde I was having some sort of hallucinations and seeing dead people. He said I had been in the funeral business a little too long and seeing corpses all of my life had been traumatizing. Granny had been in the business for over forty years. I had only been in the business for three. Something didn't add up.

Turned out, a psychic confirmed I am what was called a Betweener.

I could see ghosts of the dead who were stuck between the here and after. Of course no one but me and Jack Henry, my boyfriend and Sleepy Hollow sheriff, knew. And he was still a little apprehensive about the whole thing.

"I'm fine," I assured Doc Clyde and looked at Cephus. "Wait." I stopped and tried to swallow what felt like a mound of sand in my mouth. My mind hit rewind and took me back to the beginning of my conversation with Cephus. "Did you say Chicken sent you?"

BED-AND-BREAKFAST MYSTERIES FROM
USA TODAY BESTSELLING AUTHOR
MARY
DAHEIM

ALL THE PRETTY HEARSES
978-0-06-135159-4

Innkeeper Judith McMonigle Flynn's husband, Joe, lands in jail after his latest surveillance job abruptly ends with an insurance fraud suspect being blown away by a .38 Smith & Wesson . . . that just *happens* to belong to Joe.

LOCO MOTIVE
978-0-06-135157-0

Harried hostess Judith McMonigle Flynn decides to join her cousin Renie on a cross-country train trip to Boston on the Empire Builder. But when the train collides with a truckload of sugar beets, stranding the cousins in Middle-of-Nowhere, Montana, they soon have two murders on their hands.

VI AGRA FALLS
978-0-06-135155-6

Judith McMonigle Flynn's worst nightmare comes true when Vivian Flynn—husband Joe's first wife—moves back into the neighborhood. Vivian plans to build a big, bad condo on their idyllic cul-de-sac, attracting more than one mortal enemy. But which one ended up dead in Vivian's back yard?

GONE WITH THE WIN
978-0-06-208989-2

Judith and Cousin Renie venture into Judith's old neighborhood to track down a killer intent on seeing them come in dead last.